Anna Stothard spent her childhood in London and Washington, DC. She has attended a variety of schools and wrote a weekly column for the *Observer* when she was sixteen. Anna is starting Oxford University in autumn 2003. *Isabel and Rocco* is her first book.

Isabel and Rocco

Anna Stothard

ARROW

Published by Arrow Books in 2003

3 5 7 9 10 8 6 4

First published in the United Kingdom in 2003 by Century

Arrow Books Limited
The Random House Group Limited
20 Vauxhall Bridge Road, London SW1V 2SA

Random House Australia (Pty) Limited
20 Alfred Street, Milsons Point, Sydney,
New South Wales 2061, Australia

Random House New Zealand Limited
18 Poland Road, Glenfield,
Auckland 10, New Zealand

Random House South Africa (Pty) Limited
Endulini, 5a Jubilee Road, Parktown 2193, South Africa

The Random House Group Limited Reg. No. 954009
www.randomhouse.co.uk

A CIP catalogue record for this book is available from the British Library

Papers used by Random House are natural, recyclable products made
from wood grown in sustainable forests. The manufacturing processes
conform to the environmental regulations of the country of origin

ISBN 0 09 944332 5

Typeset by SX Composing DTP, Rayleigh, Essex
Printed and bound in Great Britain by
Bookmarque, Croydon, Surrey

TO SALLY

—ᴍ—

The First Chapter

Rocco doesn't understand what I mean when I say that pleasure is polluted after the first time. I realise it can get more intense, but it doesn't get any better. Until puberty you think there is no sensation quite as physically consuming as pain. Then the first time you come under the warm fingers of a boy, the whole universe evens out. The next time might feel better, stronger, whatever, but the world doesn't shift on its axis like during time number one. As a baby you get the base layer of first times: first pain, first shit, first walk, first word, first illness, and most of them you don't even remember, then age sixteen they ignite again and everything is original. There's the first kiss, first fuck and hundreds of those lovely tense moments of anticipation, the pure resin of the moment before you find a new sensation.

The original collector's items of a person's pleasure are their first times, but Rocco refuses to measure pleasure in anything but quantity. I want to catalogue all of my first times in this book so that when I've used them up like a box of happy pills you can only get in Thailand, at least I'll be able to look back at the good, the bad, the violent and be sixteen again.

Before I begin, let me set the scene. My name is Isabel. It has been six months since my brother and I left pretty London and the playground of our first times and moved to this new city. When we first arrived here, breathless still, we found a cheap hostel in the Latin Quarter that would give us a room for a month or two. Half a year later we are still here in our tiny, smoky bedroom where I sit to catalogue my first times. Rocco doesn't approve of me writing down what I remember. He refuses to think of anything but the present and he wants to forget about what happened in London. He is adamant that me writing this down is just another thing for us to have to worry about.

I would forget, but it never really leaves my head. I'll be able to forget London once I've sorted her out in straight lines on paper. I see this diary as a collection, like a person might collect dried-out beetles and organise them onto a board with pins through their armoured thoraxes. A collector wouldn't get over his interest until the beetles were ordered and behind glass. Only then might he be able to put them in a cupboard and admit they were just another private fad. I said that to Rocco and he looked gravely at me and asked what would happen if the collector had to catalogue every beetle he knew of, each different species he came across until the bugs took over everything. I laughed.

I can't see the city out of the window, only a brick wall of the flats opposite and an alley full of rubbish against which a man is peeing. Sitting on the corner of the desk are four toy soldiers, on top of the wardrobe is an anatomical sculpture of an eye and on the bed are two red masks, all remnants of London. I can just see the linear reflection of Rocco's body as he gets changed for bed behind me, a kidney-shaped scar on his right shoulder. I've cut my hair to just below my shoulder and dyed it mahogany brown, which makes my skin look even paler than it is. I've stopped wearing contact lenses and instead bought a pair of thin-rimmed skeletal glasses. Rocco also looks different now, having cut off all his pretty, dark curls. The bones of his face look heavier, his brow and cheekbones sharper without the soft hair framing them, and his eyes are huge green saucers in his face. We both try to look very different from how we used to be. Rocco is more desperate than me to look brand new, almost obsessed with being untraceable.

*

I remember that Sunday in November when Mum and Dad argued, not for the first time. Rocco and I tried to ignore Mum's tense voice running like oiled machinery over the top of Dad's rusty, smoker's voice. Mum and Dad were incapable of taking the middle way: they seemed always to be either having sex or arguing. Dad was a short man without enormous presence, who wore tweed suits, cashmere jumpers and cufflinks embossed with other people's initials. Everything about him looked as if he'd been washed so many times that all the colour had been rubbed out. He was terribly skinny and spoke urgently with a slight stutter and had an impish face and stern eyes while Mum had softer features with large eyes and a wide mouth that split her face in two. She painted her lips bright red when going out, to the extent that Rocco and I thought she looked edible. The war memorial antiques shop they owned was a tiny red brick cave on a corner in Camden Lock, right near the damp pollution of the river, where they sold anything from pewter plates to old guns that didn't shoot. The shop smelt of gun oil, dust, wood, stagnant London water and wet bricks. It was tall like a canister or a column and when you were inside it looked like it should be dead silent because of its heaviness and the overpowering nature of the antiques and the yellow walls. Only you could always hear people tramping on the ceiling, ruining the quiet.

I was doing a handstand, my auburn hair falling over my hands and blood slipping down to my head, when Mum and Dad began to argue again downstairs. Rocco was lying sideways on his bed, smoking a cigarette and smiling, looking at me over the top of the burning embers. Rocco often did that, using pencils and cigarettes and pieces of paper to focus his eyes. Smoke trawled up and blurred his vision, so he turned the cigarette on its side and used it to watch other things in the room while I dismounted from my handstand. It was about seven o'clock and night was just slipping like a tea cosy over Camden Town. Our loft smelt of toasting hashish and perfume, but the window was open so it was breezier than usual. Rocco was eighteen, I was sixteen and we still shared a bedroom like we always had done. Rocco grinned at me, twisting a piece of floral material through his fingers with his right hand and manoeuvering the cigarette with his left. His grin is very difficult not to smile back at – very secure and steady with a slightly sarcastic edge. I tried to think of something to say that had nothing to do with Mum or Dad, but they were swearing now, words loud and sharp as bursting balloons.

Rocco and I looked at each other as Mum yelled some line of energetic abuse at Dad; the argument skipped a beat and the tempo changed, sharp as violin strings tightened out of tune. I got up from the floor and opened the loft door so we could hear more clearly. They were shouting, their sentences lapping over each other, and Rocco and I tiptoed down the stairs. We moved carefully and hovered on the stairs, hunched like we used to when we were tiny, clinging to the banisters and peeking through into the hallway. The air smelt heavily of Mum's floral perfume, as if it was sweating out of her skin, mingling with the slight stench of Dad's cigarette.

Mum and Dad loved to paint everything yellow, so the walls in the hallway were sticky yellow with a frieze of beige across the top. It was a small hallway with the front door opposite the stairs and the sitting room and kitchen doors in between. Gripping the white banister hard, I watched the theatrics below. Mum was wearing a silk dressing gown tied up with a mismatched belt that wasn't keeping it closed very effectively, and there were sweat patches under her arms. The material was static and clung to her legs, and her hair was messy around her face, with bits of it clinging to the sweat on her temples. She bit her top lip hesitantly, knocking her face off centre. Dad's white shirt was discoloured by sweat; his creased suit trousers kept up by a black belt. They stood opposite each other, mouths munching words and spitting curses, their faces liquefying and snapping, hands expressing angst and bodies sharp. The argument was about something that Dad had bought and couldn't sell. They swapped places in the hallway, moving around each other like opposing magnets trying to stay apart, and when Mum said something a little louder than the rest of the song Dad hit her sideways over her left cheek so that she fell to the floor. She let out a whimpering scream and Rocco and I got up from our hiding place and began to run down the stairs. Mum's fat lips were quivering, holding beads of sweat in the crease between her nose and mouth. That was the first time I knew of that Dad had hit her and the wet slap sound made me jump.

'Don't even think about it,' Dad said to us as I put a foot down on the hall floor and he looked so stern that I stopped dead, all my weight poised achingly on my clenched front foot, wanting to help Mum. Dad was hardly ever firm with us, so the expression looked wrong on his face. The two frown wrinkles on his forehead became pronounced, deep as knife marks. I took a step back on to the staircase and Rocco put a hand on my bare shoulder. I could feel sweat from the palm of his hand on my dry skin and we could see Mum wasn't crying although she had a neon hand-print on her salt-skidded cheek. 'Go back upstairs,' Dad said. 'And don't go sneaking about.'

'You hit her,' I said.

'You shouldn't be eavesdropping,' Dad said, and Rocco turned me around, leading me back up into the loft while Dad pawed over Mum, apologising to her softly like a baby.

—⁓—

2

Toy Soldiers

All the next day while we walked around Camden in the rain, I wore one of Dad's huge cashmere jumpers with cigarette holes in it. London is happy in the rain. In the summer it just collapses in on itself and old poisons perspire from the pores of the bricks. Heavy clothes suit the English in a way that burnt navels or sweat patches don't and everyone looked cosy walking the wet streets wrapped in their scarves and jumpers. I was wrapped up warm too, with my long black duffel coat and floppy hood over the top of the jumper, but Rocco was just wearing a shirt and black trousers because he had an amazing trick of never being cold. He used to be able to get a day off school whenever he wanted to because he always seemed to have a slight fever. Pollution is part of the Camden atmosphere, just as the seaside wouldn't be the seaside without salt air. It's not strong pollution,

just a light flavouring that pushes London forward,
lubricating the area surrounding the people as mud
would.

'You cold?' Rocco asked me. The rain was getting
harder, slapping down on the dirty London pavement
slabs with thousands of sharp cracks. I nodded and let
the cold shiver through my head and down the sides
of my spine. I had long hair down to my waist and
although Rocco and I look very different, we both
have similar green eyes.

'You wet?' I said, and he nodded enthusiastically,
letting globules of rain spin off the ends of his thick
hair as if he was momentarily head-banging to the
sound of rainfall. We walked among the oily people
towards Dad's shop and stood outside its misted-up
windows, wondering if we could somehow get inside.
The stall holders around the canal were hurrying to
put up big plastic umbrellas to shield themselves
while they packed their tables away and the sound of
wet metal against metal and stone was cacophonous,
like a metal zoo where the bird beaks were rusty.
London was a blocked sink, ugly things floating in the
creases of the road, the river twisting faster, hectic wet
people trying to get past each other. We could just see
inside the shop, which was cluttered with strange
things like a still life painting. It looked hugely heated
from our cold viewpoint on the kerb, almost tropical

and padded dark. Rocco put a hand on my head and carefully dragged a hairpin out of my hair, slipping it in and out of the keyhole, jarring around inside until he felt a satisfying click. The door swung open and we walked into the soft darkness. Rocco was good at picking locks.

It was similar to how it always was, only more messy, as if Dad didn't come in much anymore. When the shop began there were only a few antique guns and helmets mixed up with war memorial books, but now there were hundreds of guns, strange solid scalpels from war hospitals, tangles of rope, metal trunks that had held the soldiers' clothes, medals in a glass box, uniforms hanging from the beams of the ceilings, and an incongruous umbrella vase. Dad never seemed to sell anything much, so his collection increased more and more each year. I touched one of the cold guns sitting on the counter and dislodged a duvet of dust on to my damp finger, thinking how Dad used to keep the place much cleaner. It didn't look as if he'd been in here playing with his guns much recently because the room smelt too settled. Whenever he was in here he would file the sharp insides of a gun and the room would fill with metal shavings. Instead of smelling of metal and gun oil today, it smelt of dust and damp: thick, sticky and heavy. There was hardly any space on the floor and we tiptoed over the rubble.

In the corner of the room there was a bin liner full of hundreds of antique toy soldiers. They were oddly attractive, cluttered up in the dusty bag, and Rocco and I ran our hands over the men. I picked up a handful of soldiers and let them fall through my fingers. It was warm in the shop compared to the weather outside and the sharp tin was cold under my palms. I tidied my long auburn hair over my shoulder to wipe the rain and sweat from my neck. There was an accumulation of dust on the soldiers and Rocco crouched down next to the bag, sitting in a particularly severe shaft of sunlight which had appeared from outside. The rain, I noticed, seemed to be clearing up a little, the sink unblocking now we were out of it.

Dad loved lead toy soldiers, old guns and heavy metal war memorabilia more than anything else. When he was cleaning or laying out the shelves of his shop, his face would look different, like a little boy's. He'd get this cute smile on his face and an almost startled look in his eyes. He used to have some bigger toy soldiers that were much more ornate than these baby bug ones. There had only been ten of them, painted in camouflage with proper felt hats, and because Dad would let us play with almost anything we wanted from the shop, we had spent hours occupied by soldier games. He'd even play with us sometimes and give us bits of information about ammunition and tactics that we'd remember reverently: the person who shot this gun, the person who died in this helmet. It was ironic, but the thing that really made Dad look innocent was the inspiration he derived from the accessories of war.

Rocco and I felt for the sharp soldiers at the bottom of the bin liner in the corner of Dad's shop. Some of them had spears, and the tiny needles of tarnished metal poking out of the three layers of thin black plastic looked violent. Rocco crouched and fiddled with the soldiers for a couple of minutes, lost in thought. He poked them and toyed with them in his hand. He put his palm flat and arranged four of them on the curve of his flesh. Then he closed his hand and they were bundled together.

'Do you think Dad would notice if we took some?' I asked, nodding at the soldiers. There must have been about five hundred of the little men and it didn't even look as if Dad came in here anymore, so I doubted he'd notice. Rocco and I walked into Dad's office, which was clean and orderly. He had a pile of papers stacked on one side of his desk next to a ballpoint pen, and all his tools hung neatly on their pegs. I took a plastic bag from the top of the dusty filing cabinet and we carefully scooped around two hundred of the little soldiers from the dustbin bag to the shopping bag where they clattered and banged.

'What will we do with them?' I laughed and Rocco

shrugged, holding one of the men up to the light and twirling it between his thumb and forefinger. Rocco placed four carefully in his pocket while looking out of the window at the sun, which was shining now over the varnished street and the river.

There was a back entrance to the shop next to Dad's office, which had a large tarnished knob and paint peeling off like scabbed blood and, as we stood fondling the little soldiers, we heard a key in the door and a tall man in jeans and a dirty white shirt slid through into the hallway, closing the door carefully before turning around and noticing us. He had a hooked nose and small eyes hidden behind thick-rimmed glasses, which blinked twice when he saw us. His shoes trod shiny scars on to the dirty floor and he stood very still to look at us, as if he were trying to work out if we were really there.

'Hello,' Rocco and I said in unison, clarifying the matter. 'We're Jack and Kate's children,' I said. He took off his glasses and wiped the blots of rain from the lenses with the sleeve of his shirt before placing them back on his large nose and looking at us again. Mum and Dad owned our house, but they rented the shop from this man.

'I'm the landlord,' he replied carefully and took a heavy step forward, making me wonder if he did everything in an odd kind of slow motion. I'd seen him around the shop before, but we'd never spoken. He was a businessman who dealt in property and lived in the flat above the shop. I'd heard Dad complain about how untrustworthy his landlord was, so it was interesting to meet him.

'Do you two have a key to this place?' the landlord asked.

'No,' Rocco said. The man shrugged, arching his sluggish eyebrows and tensing his dry mouth. 'We picked the lock,' he said. 'Sorry, but we didn't break anything.'

'In future,' the landlord said stiffly, 'would you mind not doing that? It is breaking and entering.'

'Dad said we could have these soldiers,' Rocco lied. 'Do you mind if we take them?'

The man shrugged again and peered into the neat office where Dad used to spend most of his time. 'They're not worth anything at all,' the man said wearily, glancing back at us. 'Do you mind leaving? I have some business to attend to.'

'In here?' I asked.

'Yes, in here,' the man said. 'Could you tell your father to telephone me?'

'Sure,' Rocco said as we both walked over to the door, 'nice meeting you, we'll pass on the message.'

The man walked into the office, shutting the door unhurriedly behind him and leaving Rocco and I to disappear out of the hot shop and into the spitting rain at our leisure.

*

Mum and Dad were in the kitchen when we walked into the hallway, dripping wet and holding the bag of Dad's soldiers. They were sitting opposite each other with plates of cold ham, salad and pitta bread between them on the table. Mum was eating hers hungrily while Dad pushed his food from one side of the plate to the other. They were talking and laughing, Dad frowning when he spoke and Mum teasing him. Dad had been ill with flu for the last fortnight, and he didn't look very well at all. He had big shadows under his eyes and skin the colour that paper goes when it's left out in the rain and then dried on top of a radiator. He was always tired looking.

Dad's eyes lit up slightly when he saw us and his tight little dry mouth half-smiled deeper into his face while Mum turned around in her chair to greet us. They had the lamps dimmed down, but even in the frosted light I could see that Dad's right eye was twitching lazily. Mum turned back to Dad and put her hand over his, wrapping one of her fingers under his thumb.

'Did you have a good day?' Mum asked, her back to us.

'Fine thanks, we went to the shop,' I replied and watched Dad's smile limp slightly between his thin cheeks.

'How did you get in?' Dad asked. He cocked his head heavily in our direction and Rocco ran his hand along the dado line that went around the kitchen, collecting dust on his finger.

'With Isabel's hair clip,' Rocco smiled, and I felt sad because his was such a sweet, nervous smile and neither Mum nor Dad smiled back. If anything, their frowns got deeper. 'We found some little soldiers,' Rocco continued, 'Do you mind if we have them?'

'Of course not, they're not worth anything,' Mum said. 'Just some stupid things Dad wasted a bit of money on last month. I doubt we'll sell any of them. Do you want some food?'

Rocco put down the bag of soldiers with a clatter in the doorway while I put the kettle on, then we sat down on either side of Mum at the table. She smiled at both of us, and then at Dad. I saw that she squeezed his yellowing hand gently with her pretty fingers. Mum had pale hair, with red lips and a sudden smile. There was a merriment about her and a recklessness. For someone so tidy, her taste in clothes was erratic and she wore strange combinations. One day a long skirt and a sweater, another day tight trousers and a bright green t-shirt.

'We met the landlord,' I said after an awkward silence – Rocco, like always, wasn't bothering to make conversation with Mum and Dad. Mum was watching Dad's hand, looking dazed. Rocco wasn't getting on all that well with Mum and Dad anymore. He used to be a very quiet, beautiful child with these slippery green eyes that would watch and think without showing any emotion, but he seemed to make Mum quite uncomfortable, particularly as he got older. He has this presence as if the air is denser around him than it is around other people. He would look so concentrated that you couldn't help wondering what the solid little boy was thinking. Rocco was also strong, stronger than Mum and Dad were. The idea of anyone looking after him was embarrassing.

Rocco was a lot quieter around Mum and Dad than he is around me. When we were younger we used to sneak through the house, because it was fun to play spies and war. We'd listen to their arguments and catalogue their love-making on scrappy bits of paper that we'd hide under Rocco's bed, making sure nobody saw us. We watched them kiss, watched them laugh, watched them shout. We'd collect dried bugs from behind curtains and keep them in boxes then splat them under the plain pages of exercise books, giving them fairy names because the way their wings splayed out and their bodies burst, they looked like squashed winged children. Rocco played up to Mum's discomfort by leaving the collections lying around or by talking about perfectly reasonable boy things – guns and insects, blood and metal – only in such a way that his monologues would make Mum nervous. Mum's soft features would become awkward, as if she didn't know how to react to her son's presence.

*

'How did you meet him?' Mum said, sharing an uncomfortable look with Dad that Rocco and I weren't meant to see. She took her hand away from Dad's.

'He came through the back door while we were in there,' I said, and looked at Dad. 'He wants you to phone,' I said to him.

'You shouldn't have gone in there really,' Mum said, reaching around to massage her own shoulders with her left hand.

'Sorry,' I replied. 'We didn't think you'd mind.'

Mum began to arrange things on the kitchen table, folding a couple of newspapers into a pile in the corner. She put the saltcellar and olive oil in line with the peppershaker, tightening their tops methodically. Her hands moved quickly, her long nails clicking against the objects while Dad sat very still.

'We didn't look through anything in your desk. We weren't nosy,' I said.

'I should hope not,' Mum said curtly, arranging her cutlery on her plate and then, thinking better of it, taking her fork up again and picking at Dad's untouched food. 'You're not ten years old, Rocco,' she said, looking at him pointedly and not at me. 'You can't do exactly what you want whenever you feel like it.'

'Although you can,' Rocco said to our father.

'What?' Dad said, waking up.

'Hitting Mum,' Rocco reminded him and Dad broke into one of his coughing fits, which sounded like leather was tearing in his lungs. He held his chest and heaved, dragging in air and clutching the V-neck of his soft jumper. Some people have wind chimes outside their windows that are continually disturbed into clattery noises, but we had our father. Whenever he got agitated he would look strangled for a minute and then erupt. Those phlegmy, splintering sounds were the background sounds of our house and the breathing space for Rocco and me to think during every conversation we had with Mum and Dad. It was never something we worried about, it was just there.

'Go to your room,' Dad said shakily a few minutes later, still wheezing. 'That was none of your business, none of this is any of your business. You have to learn to stop hanging around eavesdropping and going places you know you're not meant to go.' The pupils of his eyes twitched slightly like fluttery bugs. 'You are not children anymore.'

Rocco put his head backwards and danced his eyes over our parents. 'Can we still have the soldiers?' Rocco asked with a rude smile.

'Just go to your room,' Dad said quickly.

Rocco pushed his chair back and walked out of the kitchen door, not closing it properly behind him and taking the soldiers with him.

'Sorry,' I said and sat still for a second. Then, stiffly, I followed my brother.

'My God, Isabel,' Mum snapped. 'Are you always

going to be his shadow?' Mum seemed to haul the sharp words out of her large, lethargic lips. I could feel myself blushing, so as I walked towards Rocco on the landing I stared solidly at my feet. We stood on the first floor landing, leant on the banisters and listened to Mum and Dad's almost incomprehensible conversation.

'I'm going out,' Dad said, and we heard him push his chair back, scraping it against the floor.

'No you're not. You're too tired,' Mum said, as if she was speaking to a child, but Dad walked out into the hallway and there was a long silence.

Then Dad said in a slow, hoarse, frightening voice, 'If you fucking kids are standing on the landing, you can stop creeping about now. Your mother and I are going out.'

Rocco and I raised our eyebrows, smiled with surprised looks at each other and did as we were told, edging our way up to our safe loft and leaving our confusing parents to their business.

—ᴍ—

CONFUSED

Three days before Dad left I walked into the sitting room where he was on the sofa with his back half facing the wall, hunched over and smoking a cigarette with slow elastic movements that made even the smoke look sluggish. There was a spliff in the ashtray, so I suppose he was stoned. I never liked our sitting room because it was full of oppressive objects that hadn't sold in the shop. There was a set of creepy blown eggs painted with purple and gold leaf kept in an Italian bowl, like eggs in a nest from a fairy story. There were glazed plates hanging from the yellow walls, a picture of the Virgin Mary, and a set of tacky ink pots reflecting light in hundreds of directions from the top of the mantelpiece. The short antique coffee table in front of the sofa had hardback books on cooking, cutlery and guns. There were also two

ancient shotguns with cement up their pipes sitting
on a tray in the middle of the table and a waxy green
plant in a coloured pot. I stood in the doorway and he
can't have heard me because he didn't look up. He had
huge shadows like bruises under his eyes and his skin
looked fractured under the pressure of small
movements, small smiles, blinks, frowns. He seemed
to have turned into a teenager again, smoking his gear
lethargically; all his movements appeared tiresome or
demanding, and he'd even developed a fine scatter of
lumpy red acne on the bottom of both his cheeks.

'Dad,' I said to signify my presence, but he still
didn't answer and continued to suck on his cigarette.
The first time I tried a cigarette I was surprised it
wasn't sweet and didn't understand why anybody
would get addicted to such an ashy, papery taste. He
stubbed it out in the saucer on the table but still didn't
look up until I went and stood in front of him and
then, slow as a tractor, he lifted up his head and
acknowledged his daughter hovering awkwardly above
the sofa. The room smelt sour and sweaty. The first
time I ever heard Mum and Dad argue was on a warm
spring day when they decided to make a herb garden,
but couldn't agree on anything so Mum ended up
storming through the house leaving a trail of mud
behind her on the carpets. Now parental imperfection
has a habit of making me remember the smell of wet
soil. I wasn't sure quite what I wanted to say to Dad,

he seemed so tired and worn.

'Do you want some coffee?' I said eventually. He shook his head so I had no reason to stay in the sitting room staring curiously at my aging father. Instead I went into the kitchen, where Mum was unwrapping fish and chips from their greasy paper packets, but she didn't want to have a conversation either. She was wearing black trousers and a black polo neck, her hair loose and framing her tight face. She kept burning herself on the steam and the kitchen smelt of Brighton, except hotter and she was half-watching a chat show on the TV although she didn't have the sound on. All you could see were these girls in skimpy clothes standing opposite each other, clicking their fingers and making huge liquid oval shapes with their red lips. They looked like balls of excess energy, all their limbs snapping apart from their bodies and their big breasts bouncing as they argued.

'What are you watching?' I asked.

'I'm not really watching it,' she said and shrugged. 'I bought Rocco and you some chips,' she said, and pushed a greasy packet across the table.

'Thanks,' I said, smiling, but she just frowned.

'I'm going to go and give this to your father,' she said and left me sitting in the kitchen eating fat chips and watching the silent television. I could hear what Mum and Dad were saying quite plainly, each word unsure from their lips, negative, empty sentences but as aggressive as gaseous energy. It wasn't physical, just potent words I chose to ignore and made my way upstairs instead to share my chips with Rocco.

They hadn't always been like this. Mum used to be great fun when she chose to be, only her eyes were deeper set in her face now. She used to let us have sips of her vodka and tonic when we went out to dinner and she'd get the giggles at inappropriate times as I always do. My most vivid memory of her is during our last family holiday when I was eleven and Rocco was thirteen. We went to Malta, with its surreal grey slabs like poured concrete instead of beaches, and stayed in a little hotel without air conditioning. We had a lovely time, filled with picnics on the rocks and unsuccessful shopping trips in the village.

Breakfast at the hotel was in a canteen-style room that you could only get to through an ancient lift, and everything served was greasy or burnt. I think that I'll always choose to remember Mum's face as it was the morning when she persuaded Dad to let us have breakfast in a café and, instead of ordering us cornflakes, the waiter brought us this huge luminous blue ice cream with strawberries and cream. She just looked so amused and happy, not even getting angry when Rocco tried to flick a strawberry at me with his spoon and got cream all over my new dress. Dad was always different; never stern, but in general aloof with us a lot of the time. He'd correct our manners and look the other way if Rocco told rude jokes or I knocked over glasses. He was strict on etiquette and didn't particularly like being touched. He seemed very intelligent to us, and sometimes when he talked I simply went blank and just pretended I was listening to his lecture.

It annoyed Dad when I put on this vacant look when he talked, desperately batting off his clever words or simply letting them pass cleanly through me. He wanted Rocco and I to have better chances than he did, better morals and better prospects. I think that perhaps we disappointed him, because at some point he stopped caring quite so much. Mum stopped brushing my hair in the morning, Dad stopped lecturing me, they were annoyed a lot and I think they lost their optimism. It was their tiredness that was amazing. Food, the shop, the house, the bills, the children. It was all attacked in the same lethargic manner. Only when they touched each other was there some hint of energy. I know now that Dad did something wrong, solidifying their flowery characters and inking more wrinkles into their skin. I miss them now we're so far away and I'd do anything for things to have turned out differently.

When Dad did eventually leave we were offered very little explanation, but the memory of him hunched in the sitting room, ignoring me, stuck in my mind. Mum told us over dinner on Thursday night. We came through the door and she was resting her head on her arm, leaning across the table. The dining room table was set with our navy blue china plates and matching gravy boat. The light was powdery grey from the clouds outside the window and a pollen light echoed off the candles. I stood in the doorway and Rocco stood behind my shoulder.

'Hello kids,' she said sadly, hauling herself up into a more conventional dinner position. Adding to the confusion of her face was the crease her jumper had left on her cheek, giving her the strange appearance of a badly hung clotheshorse. She wasn't wearing her glasses and she had mole eyes, little origami slits in her crumpled skin. Her mouth sat heavily in her face, set in a slight pout. She had obviously been waiting for us and I felt terribly sorry because she looked pathetically tired, and according to Rocco, obviously drunk. She'd been so beautiful when she was younger, as she would often boast, and all the men had been in love with her.

'Sorry we're late,' I said cautiously, watching her slow, balletic movements. 'We didn't know you were cooking.'

'Oh, you weren't to know. It's a bit cold, but do you want some?' She looked up hopefully at us. Her make-up was slipping off her face and I could see her wrinkles underneath. I wondered if wrinkles, like scars, were your body's way of keeping score. An indentation after an illness, a death, a broken heart, failed ambition, sadness. All built up into wrinkles, masked but not hidden under liquid foundation.

'Sure, sure. I'm really hungry actually. And chicken is good cold,' I said, sounding disjointed, and we sat down at the table.

'Chicken?' Mum slurred. She carved a jagged lump of breast meat off for me, concentrating ceremoniously at placing it on my plate. It lay white in the middle of the blue china plate, looking like a sheep curled up in a foetal position in a field of blue flowers. Then she took a spoonful of gravy and drowned my lump. Mum looked nervous and old in the grey and yellow light. She ripped a leg off the chicken with her hands and put it on Rocco's plate, then wiped the varnished grease from her fingers on to a napkin. Rocco smiled at me, half-amused to see our mother wasted and half as an act of reassurance. I wasn't reassured, actually I had a nauseous, knotted feeling in my stomach.

'So . . .' Mum said, trailing off. 'Good day?'

'Yeah,' I said.

'Do anything?' she asked. Rocco took his cigarettes from the pocket of his trousers and lit one, smoking it languidly with one elbow on the table and fixing his smoke-screened eyes on Mum.

'Not really,' I said. Rocco turned his chicken around

and pushed it to the side of his plate. I cut a piece of mine and put it in my mouth, but it was lukewarm and the gravy was bitter.

'Um, Mum?' I began. 'Where's Dad?' Mum looked at Rocco and me.

'I wanted to talk to you about that,' she said stiffly, trying to keep her syllables together coherently. She paused and looked at Rocco, who was sitting still as a clockwork animal.

'Dad has gone away . . . on holiday.' She took a sip of wine and fiddled with the napkin next to her plate, running the corners through the soft skin between her fingers just like I did with my duvet.

'He's left you,' I said, and she looked surprised. She wiped her face with her hand, smudging her foundation in streaks. My body felt floppy and my eyelids heavy, almost aching for Mum not to look so weary. Distractedly she wrapped her hair around her fingers and looked up at me sharply. 'Your father isn't very well. He's gone away to get better.' I felt passive and featureless, almost numb. She looked sad.

'What's wrong with him?' I asked nervously.

'He's exhausted,' she said after a moment's hesitation. 'You'll have to stay on your own for a while,' she tried to smile. 'I have to go to look after him. You'll be OK here, won't you?'

'Sure,' I said trying to make my voice sound level and calm.

'You're always provoking your father and me,' Mum said, looking more at Rocco than me. 'I just can't stay here when your father needs me elsewhere.'

'Mum, it's fine, go, we'll be fine,' I said, and tried to touch her hand, but she recoiled from me and Rocco and I took the gesture as a cue to leave the room. It wasn't the fact that they were leaving that worried me, they often went on holiday without us, it was the sad look in her eyes.

'It's not my fault,' Mum said as we got up. 'It's his fault.'

I had this horrible thought that I understood even less now than I did when I was ten. When children light a match they deduce that fire is yellow and hot, and that it burns their skin. They learn that metal won't ignite, plastic melts and teacups break. They cut themselves and a parent explains that every little girl and boy has metallic tasting redness inside them. There is no real sense of tomorrow or yesterday, but only the moment that the body exists in, until all these complications occur and slowly you understand less and less.

I looked back at Mum as we left the dining room and she was staring at us through blocks of tears. I smiled at her and, because of her tears, she didn't smile back. If it is the case that you only get more confused as you lose your innocence, then no wonder Mum and Dad looked so sad and baffled most of the time.

4

—ᴍ—

MUM AND DAD

Mum and Dad's room is just below the loft and I
remember the first time we heard them having sex. I
was almost six years old and we were playing games
with toy masks up in the loft when this strangled
sound came from downstairs. I was standing on my
bed, my feet muddled up inside the creases of the
warm sheets and the cold paper of a mask over my hot
face. Dad had bought us the burgundy-coloured
masks for Christmas one year and we adored them,
making them the centre of most of our carefully
planned games. They scared Mum because when we
wore them the snouts made us look like big
mosquitoes, which she hated.

Rocco was kneeling on the floor holding his mask in
his hand and waving it at me to make me giggle, when
we heard strange noises downstairs. There was

laughter that also sounded like crying and as we pricked up our ears their bed began to creak methodically. Dad shouted something at Mum, who started to gasp out for breath and I imagined Dad was trying to strangle her.

As Dad's shouts got louder they almost shook the house so we jumped up and rushed gallantly downstairs on our chubby feet to save Mum, bursting into their bedroom with our mosquito masks strapped boldly over our faces. Mum was naked and Dad had his shirt on, pushing her up against the back of the bed as if he was trying to become her, as if he never wanted to be away from her ever again. Like if you had two playdoh sculptures and you squashed them together until they became one mushy ball. Their bodies were shiny and white with similar chaotic abandonment to that of hysterical giggles or temper. After that we used to go to sleep every night with the radio on, but in the few years before Dad left, the noises had pretty much stopped, possibly because Dad had been getting flu a lot.

When Dad got flu the whole house would smell of disinfectant, Lemsip and tea for a week. Mum would buy huge amounts of food from the supermarket that Dad wouldn't eat and she'd clean the house obsessively. It was in these hushed times, while Rocco and I tiptoed about the house, that it really became clear to us how much Mum loved Dad. They argued a lot usually, but when he got ill Mum devoted herself to him, moving through the lemon-scented silence like a paper doll. She was always the kind of person who cleaned the house a lot and put things away where they were meant to be, but when Dad was ill she became fanatical about doing the laundry and cooking food. She put on weight, wore brighter lipstick and tied her hair back tight against her face. The last time it happened, about three weeks before he left, Mum made proper meals, fresh bread that Dad would nibble on and leave, fairy cakes that piled up in a bowl on the kitchen table and real cups of coffee ground from a little machine she kept for special occasions. The rooms would smell warm as a country cottage and only Dad's cool voice reminded us that we lived in angular London streets.

Rocco and I were never allowed to see him while he was ill in bed, but we sometimes heard him making a scene or groaning that he wanted to get up while Mum purred at him and told him everything was going to be all right. We spent most of the time out of the house during those weeks because we seemed to be in the way, but when we did meet her on the stairs or in the kitchen she would be carrying trays of tea and toast up to Dad, arranged neatly like a religious feast, with a thermometer in her hands and a tea towel over her arm. In those weeks the divide between them and us became more apparent, an almost physical barrier that made even basic conversation difficult. We'd have monosyllabic conversations – 'off out', 'turn off the TV' – as if we were tapping Morse code across a desert. When Mum did talk to us, there was a creepy feeling that she was looking through us. She loved him, I understand that now, and to her we were indifferent bystanders.

In retrospect, the last time it happened it seemed to be more serious than previous episodes. Rocco and I were up in the loft listening to music when we heard something crash down in Dad's room. Things were always crashing in our house, so we rarely took much notice. Rocco stayed sitting down on the floor, not even looking up from his book.

'Did you hear that?' I said and he shook his head, lying. I opened the door and something else crashed, making a splintering, fractured sound so I ran down the stairs. Just as I was darting towards the door, Mum must have been running up the stairs in the same blind, anxious state that I was in and neither of us saw each other in time so we collided, sending her tray of food tumbling back down the stairs. I tried to grab the falling things in the same movement that I bumped into her, but caught nothing, watching it instead as it jumped and splattered over the stairs.

'Sorry,' I said and she didn't say anything. 'I'll clean it up.'

She didn't look at me or the spilt lunch, but opened

the door to their bedroom and slid through the crack, letting out a musky, ill smell into the clean hallway for a moment. I began to clean up the mess with a dustpan and brush from downstairs, listening to Mum's comforting voice talking to Dad as he coughed and grumbled. My hands were shaking as I shifted the splinters of china and soggy, bright yellow scrambled egg from the floor.

'Don't worry, Isabel,' she said, slipping her head out of the door. 'I'll do it in a minute. There's ten pounds on the kitchen table, why don't you and Rocco go out? There's no point in everyone being stuffed up in this house.' Her heavy lips dragged across her face with a forced smile and I nodded as she closed the door. I finished brushing up the mess anyway, because I felt bad about leaving it there and then Rocco and I went out to the cinema, pleased to find that when we got home everything was quiet and clean again.

Upstairs in the loft after eating cold chicken and bitter gravy with Mum, I thought about all these things, but nothing clicked. Rocco and I sat in silence for a few moments and then he went down to take a shower. When I was left alone, the house felt silent and empty: not a tranquil quiet, but the cluttered silence that only city houses produce. Superficially, it was hushed as I padded around the loft, but when I listened deeper there were cars fizzing outside, deeper than that and I could hear people coming out of the pub and, if it was possible to listen still deeper, there were probably birds and dogs, and factories whirring and newspaper presses creaking all around. There were probably people making love in houses nearby, washing machines bubbling, babies crying, fog rising and dew settling over the bricks of London, but all I could hear was my feet on the carpet.

It was about eight thirty and the clouds had a blue tint as the earth began to haul its leaden body in front of the sun. I picked up one of Rocco's pre-rolled cigarettes between my long fingers and reached for his lighter, which was on the window ledge. As I lit the cigarette I glanced out of the window and saw the shadow of a man, also smoking a cigarette, leaning on the wall at the corner. His hand moved up and down from his mouth stiffly. Around him, London looked like a shantytown or a stage set, bricks pretending to be buildings propped up by damp card and lined with rusty corrugated iron. In case the man saw me looking at him I stepped nervously to the left of the window and without putting the lights on I shut the blinds.

I picked up a biological sculpture of a human eye that Rocco kept next to his bed; he had stolen it from Dad's antique shop a couple of years ago. It was very beautifully made out of painted wood with all the layers and bits slotting together exactly. There were no spaces between the different anatomical sections and apparently it was exactly like a real eye except it had calligraphy labels for each bit like the iris, the cornea and the pebble-round pupil. I didn't get the same feeling that Rocco did about the sculpture. I saw it for exactly what it was, a rather old piece of medical teaching equipment that had probably spent most of its life in a bleach-white cabinet staring out at practical surgery and bored biology students, but I assume Rocco saw it as art.

When Rocco was younger he wanted to be a doctor, only he was scared of blood. Age five I fell off a swing and slit my little wrist on glass, hitting an artery so that blood spewed out everywhere, soaking my chubby fist like a sponge. Rocco came over from the tyre to the swings to see why everyone was crowding around. I wasn't crying at this point and I raised my bloody hand in a kind of half wave in Rocco's direction, spitting wads of blood from my hand that landed on his face. He looked shocked for a second, began raising his arm – either in recognition or to wipe his face – and then toppled over sideways on to the cork mats.

He didn't mind his own blood, but other people's disgusted him. When he talked about the human body he would get this brightness in his eyes. Not in a particularly sexual way, but just an inspired, interested way because he loved the way it slotted together in a perfectly organised system with everything snug in its jigsaw place and with its specific job. He once told me that blood stood for disorder and Rocco hated disorder. He kept facts and figures in one cabinet inside his head, ideas in another, plans in another, liking to know the structure of everything he was doing. He loved the idea of chaos, but didn't want to be part of it. I don't hate blood, actually I'm very partial to the colour red. I had a brief love affair with blue because I liked the colour of swimming pools, but was ultimately reconverted back to the colour of tongues and lips. When you close your eyes and picture an emotion, all the good ones are Ottoman carpet red.

The silence was buzzing in my ears so I turned on the television. We had somehow managed to break the aerial, so we didn't get all the channels and I left it on a nature programme where two gem-green beetles, one male and one female, were guarding an armoured legion of silver babies. They were all in a cave, scurrying blindly around and bumping into each other. The light from the screened window was soft as putty and the green-tinted light from the television flickered over the loft floor, which was still tiled haphazardly with tin soldiers. They reflected the light and scattered it. The end of the cigarette burnt shiny as a glow-worm and as I sucked in the smoke I felt slightly comforted. I watched the pretty beetles scurry for a few moments before I heard Rocco on the stairs.

Rocco and I have always liked insects. They have a
kind of dumb, ephemeral beauty and the fact that they
have no backbone seems practical. Backbones are so
designed and sculpted with all those puzzle pieces
fitting together that you could almost base an entire
argument for the existence of God on their artistic
perfection. It's such an important bit of the body,
holding everything up, yet it's so thin. It's like having
an ivory twig down your back. I wondered whether
when you broke your neck your head tumbled to one
side. The body might be a machine that fits together
prettily as Rocco enthused, but it does break very
easily. Insects don't have backbones and they are the
most successful creatures in the animal kingdom.
Dragonflies are my favourite, because for some reason
they haven't evolved, so were the same three hundred
million years ago when they would have flown with
the same taut veined wings. The largest dragonfly ever
known is a fossilised specimen from America with a
wingspan of sixty centimetres, but most are small as
delicate jewellery. Rocco was always industriously
researching how insects made love because, after
seeing Mum and Dad at it, we were struck by the idea
that it simply didn't look practical. Male damselflies,
insects similar to dragonflies, transfer their sperm to a
structure of the lower surface of the abdomen, near
their back legs. They clasp the female's neck using the
tip of their abdomen and the female then raises her

own abdomen to collect the sperm. They fly together in this tandem position for some time, often forming a heart shape with the male's head down at the tip and the female head at the tip of the heart.

—ɱ—

MUM LEAVES

The next morning Mum left to look after Dad. She stood next to a suitcase in the hallway to say goodbye to us, red rims around her eyes bringing attention to the dampness of her skin. She smiled and we stood awkwardly in front of her, Rocco leaning on the wall and me shifting from foot to foot as we spoke.

'Sorry I was rude last night,' she said. 'I promise that when we get back everything will be peaceful again. Only you have to understand that I don't feel like explaining just now.'

I nodded dumbly and Rocco looked around the hall as Mum continued.

'You two are adults now,' she said, trying to pin up her hair, which was falling down over her face. 'We've all got into bad habits and you don't tell us your problems either. It's not just us being bad parents.

When we get back we'll start again and all be friends.'
Her words were stilted and nervous.

'How long will you be gone?' I asked, and Mum
looked weary.

'It depends on Dad,' she said. 'I've left you some
money in your bank accounts. I'm sorry it's not much.
One of the neighbours is going to come and check up
on you every so often.'

'Sure,' I said. 'Give Dad our love, I hope he gets
better.'

'He will,' she said. 'And when we get back it will be
like nothing ever happened. We'll just forget all this
and get back to normal.'

Rocco picked up Mum's bag and carried it to the
taxi outside, but I stayed in the doorway because I
didn't have any socks on and when I hugged her she
felt bony, full of sharp edges. I thought she might turn
to powder when I touched her because she looked like
a delicate old doll that hadn't been moved in
generations, but she stayed intact, even seeming to
soften a little for a moment. When she broke away
from the hug she looked at me and I thought for a
second that she might ask me to go with her to see
Dad, but then she looked at the floor.

'It'll all be better in a couple of weeks,' she assured
me.

'Remember to give him our love,' I said. 'And tell
him we're sorry.'

'Of course,' she replied, and Rocco came back, kissing Mum on the cheek to say goodbye before she walked to the taxi, her blonde hair unpinning again as she rushed.

After the door slammed, Rocco and I stood in the small hallway, not talking, but looking at the yellow walls and Mum's winding pot plant sitting in the corner. The house felt drained of energy. I imagined it a huge origami house, with flimsy brittle walls and rising damp. I touched the walls lightly with my fingers and they did feel like paper, slightly rough and treated. Without Mum or Dad's argumentative music shrilling from any rooms, Rocco and I were padded in by this wonderful household hush. We listened to her get in the taxi and heard the taxi rev its engine as it pulled out into the streets, leaving Rocco and me hovering in the yellow hallway of the empty house. I looked at the sitting room door and, through the ruler crack, I could see a little bit of the coffee table with two ink pots on top of some magazines. The house was a collection of antiques without the collectors, just like the shop had seemed to become once Dad stopped going there. Rocco leaned on the wall and lit a cigarette as if he was moving on tiptoe, and I was aware of every shadow and breath in the house. The hallway was as bad as the supermarket car park at night. I could hear Rocco sucking in the smoke and, even though Mum and Dad leaving was not out of the ordinary, I felt oddly apprehensive. I suppose it was the way she said that she left money.

'You hungry?' I said eventually.

'Sort of,' Rocco replied.

—ɯ—

GIRLS AND BOYS

I'd only slept without Rocco in the room once in my life, aged ten, a night after taking my clothes off to go in the sprinkler. I was alone in the garden playing with my dolls and, although it was seven o'clock, the summer had prolonged the light and the heat. Bored of dolls, I turned on the sprinkler and watched the needles of water prick the air in the little garden, splashing against the leaves of our tree and against the red bricked walls on either side. We had a small concrete statue of a cat with green gem eyes that sat underneath the tree, and two stone geese, one with a broken neck sitting next to its severed head. They both got wet underneath the sprinkler, but neither moved.

I chewed on the sleeve of my linen dress. I was quite a fidgety child, who did everything too quickly for fear of disappearing over the side of the earth before I'd got everything done. I was always making trouble by mistake and not understanding what was going on around me. I got hot underneath my skin as I watched the stringy water jump up and down like a billion lemmings, so I stood over the sprinkler to let the water gush up between my thighs. The material was sticky, clinging to my armpits and skin. I put my hands out and closed my eyes as if I was a bird in a fountain, hovering motionlessly with the pressure between my legs, but Mum shouting at Rocco broke this moment of tranquillity.

I opened my eyes with a start and looked up at our house. Rocco was leaning out of one window, full of an oddly premature dignity like Christopher Robin. Mum was looking out of another window, shouting across to Rocco. He looked slightly shocked, almost guilty, and that night Mum made Rocco sleep on the sofa. I didn't understand why there was all this commotion and for hours I sat up in my bed hugging the duvet to my chin in the warmth. Our house is attached to other houses on either side and I thought I could hear people through the walls, as if they were slowly chiselling away at the plaster with the back end of a spoon so that they could sneak in and steal me away while I was asleep.

Believe it or not, I started my period that night, so unnaturally early that I hadn't had any sort of sex education lessons yet. I was in a terrible mood, all the sheets were sweaty, my neck hot under my hair and the covers wouldn't fall right over my skin. When I woke up the next morning my thighs were wet, sliding against each other and as I wriggled my body awake I thought for a moment that I'd wet myself. Then I looked under the covers and there was warm blood staining the bone white sheets. I threw the duvet off and checked myself for some huge gashing wound before jumping away from the horrible sheets as if the blood was fire. I tried to muffle my tears, innately embarrassed by the smearings of blood, but Rocco had sneaked up to the loft some time in the night and he rushed over to me from his bed. When he saw the blood his face went white and he asked 'what have you done?' in a twitchy voice, looking ill. I was so glad that he was there.

'Nothing,' I whimpered, moving away from the polluted bed and holding on tight to Rocco's wrist. He scanned me up and down, noting dried blood scabbing over the inside of my legs, but seeing no great wound. Rocco nervously got out one of his school biology books and eventually, over half an hour of tears later, he worked out where the blood came from. Hot from the exhilaration of crying, I gave him a look of total shock and confusion before running down the stairs and locking myself in the toilet. I washed and examined myself, convinced this was a way to suck out my innocence and dry me into an adult. I dreamt for

weeks that my insides were actually full of larvae and
I was just their house, only nobody had got round to
explaining this to me yet. I imagined all the larvae
sitting on my heart and copulating inside my womb,
jostling each other, ready to turn into caterpillars and
eat me inside out. There are types of mosquitoes that
inject their eggs under animal skin, where the babies
hatch and eat the muscle of their host. Or even worse,
the tarantula hawk, the world's largest moth. The
female of the species captures a spider and paralyses
it with her sting. She then lays an egg on its
motionless body while it is still alive and pushes it into
a burrow so that when the eggs hatch they can feed on
the fresh spider meat.

After the period incident, Rocco's and my interest
in blood made a comeback. No well-adjusted adult
would admit to finding blood beautiful, even though it
is a perfect and compelling colour. What Mum was
always getting annoyed about was the way that Rocco
and I would clutch on to one thought for weeks on
end. There is the outside world, the crust of the city
with all its social obligations and conformities.
Underneath this, all the different people with all their
different purposes and fetishes stay behind walls and
disarrange and rearrange their world. Each person
isn't a simple creation of *Playboy*, wanting whips and
leather, or the *Economist*, excited by shares, so there
is middle ground, strange ground, blue, grey and pale

red ground behind walls that nobody talks about for fear of upsetting the careful balance of the outside city.

I went to school that day a little dazed after Mum had left to look after Dad, but the structure of my day went on as usual. I ate some toast, grabbed my school bag and Rocco and I walked through early morning Camden towards my school and his work. It was a crisp morning and all the tramps were breaking out of their cocoons to yawn and curse from doorways. in winter, London looks as if the only liquid in it is bird droppings and spilt petrol. The trees are bare, the leaves crumble and the streets feel like the inside of cold bones.

Rocco didn't go to school anymore but worked in a pet shop during the day, selling spiders and lizards. He spent his lunch breaks hanging around Camden's dusty bookshops, never buying anything. That night he was doing a shift at the pub, so he wouldn't be home till after eleven. At the tall school gates I kissed him on the side of his mouth before walking over the barren concrete playground to the group of people in my year who hung about at the bench. The school is made out of concrete. There are two flat modern buildings, one red brick and the other smooth cigarette ash grey, separated by a slab called a playing field that isn't large enough for any known sport.

Connecting the two buildings is a walkway roofed in corrugated iron, with metal bars that the younger kids used to swing on before it got banned. The school cafeteria is a dank basement full of hexagon tables that fold up and as a result never stay up, the music rooms are a mosaic of small square prison spaces adorned with broken pianos that can't hit high notes. At the back behind the science block there is a pond that smells of chemicals, frogspawn and cigarettes, where teachers never go. A tall fence surrounds the whole school so that from almost every classroom window you are always sure to get a blocked view fencing you in from every angle.

At lunch I went straight to the music rooms and chose the largest box at the end of the corridor, with a reasonably pleasant view of the edge of the concrete playground and part of the stairs leading down to the bike shed. I perched my music on the stand and unlocked my flute from its heavy black case, fondling the different sections. The flute was slippery on the outside and tarnished and tight at the joints, only fitting together grudgingly into one thin hollow twig. I put the cold metal to my mouth and blew, making a shrill airy sound because I hadn't played it all week. Outside the window I could see my boyfriend Jackson and our group of friends sitting cross-legged in the corner of the concrete. Jackson was a tall boy whose trousers were always too loose and his shirt always untucked. He had very white skin, almost transparent, and ashy hair. Underneath the shirt, his silver studded belt was usually just visible and he wore a piece of leather with one bead around his neck. Jackson and my brother were very different looking. Rocco was steady and structured with big shoulders, strong bones, thick hair and olive skin. He spoke purposefully and had amused eyes. Jackson was tall and thin: nothing about him was structured, but gangly and slightly awkward. He was very popular, but I can't say I ever really understood him, which was perhaps part of his allure. He dragged his feet when he walked and never looked anywhere but straight in front of him.

The school uniform is black skirts and tights with see-through yellow blouses for the girls, and black trousers, yellow shirts and black and yellow-striped ties for the boys, and we always felt slightly absurd wearing them, like overgrown city bumblebees. The paint was chipping from the window frame and the glass looked greasy and un-kept, giving the room a depressing taste. The scene took a turn for the worse when I noticed Jackson, whom I'd been seeing for three months, share a glance and a quick smile with another girl in the group. I felt oddly jealous of that smile and I turned away from the window, feeling a bit like a spy up in my mousy music room looking down on them, so I put the cold silver to my lips again and began to play.

When Rocco was at school last year it was fine, but

after he was expelled I began to spend most of my time
in the small warm music room practising my flute. He
got expelled because one day, in the middle of summer
we were all playing a half-hearted game of volleyball
with somebody's jumper tied up into a knot and the
jumper got lodged on the roof of the corrugated iron
walkway. We tried to get it down with a stick, but
eventually Rocco hauled himself up one of the bars on
to the roof to throw the jumper down. Only once he
was up, he decided to remain sitting on the roof and
the headmaster came out of the science block and saw
Rocco playing catch with me from the dangerous
height of the roof. It said on his exclusion form that he
was being removed 'for potentially causing himself or
others some bodily harm, and suspected drug usage.'

I laughed when I read that, which was bad because
it was quite serious. After all the rules he'd broken at
that school – drugs taken by the pond, fences escaped
over, work ignored – he was eventually expelled for
playing volleyball with a jumper. I always tend to
laugh when serious things happen; quite disturbing
giggle fits, which come over me a little like anger that
I can't stop. The first serious giggle fit of my life
happened after our grandfather's funeral where
aggressive laughter came out sharp and fast with a lot
of spitting and spluttering because I was trying to stop
myself. Luckily it wasn't during the service, but
afterwards when everybody had moved out of the

crematorium and on to this huge stone slab mourning area where the headstones and flowers were. Not a church, because our family wasn't religious, but a factory-looking chapel. His headstone was new black marble with gold embossed words like the front of a thriller book. Around it were pretty wreaths and flowers, all bundled and colourful with bits of ribbon. As people were beginning to drift off into the car park, me included, I turned around to see Mum laden with wreaths, carrying them back to the car. Then Mum made Dad go back to the grave and pick up more wreaths. She was walking along with flowers spewing out behind her like confetti, shouting: 'Go pick up some wreaths darling, we might as well keep them.'

The giggles began with just spluttering. Once, twice, spluttering and really straining my tummy not to let out any of the bubbles of giggles. I could feel them collecting just under my lungs. Then the laughter just fell out of me and as it continued I doubled up over myself. I couldn't breathe, but I could smell my mother's French perfume nearby mixed with the smell of flowers. I thought I was going to faint and I had a really sour, sick airy feeling in my head so I sat down, heaving with helium giggles, on the tarmac floor. Mum was saying, 'Stop it, you're at a funeral. Why on earth are you laughing? Everybody is staring,' but this only reminded me that I was laughing at a funeral, and I laughed more until it hurt. Eventually I stopped and we got in the car and drove home, where nobody mentioned the episode. Everyone assumed it was just an odd manifestation of grief, which I suppose it was, but it made me wonder what laughter was, if it could occur instead of tears.

Jackson walked home with me after school and we talked about silly things, gossip at school, work we hadn't done. Camden has the messy atmosphere of a child's collage, but one made of smells and people. There are patches of Camden atmosphere smelling of cigarettes, then curry, then Thai food, then sweat. Even at night the box-shaped shops lining the pavement spew shoes and old dresses in front of them and everything is dirty. The people are loud, drunk and high. They push leaflets into your hands, especially at Camden Town station near the cool canal where the pink-haired ladies, drunk lesbians, friendly tramps and gothic teenagers congregate to meet their friends. There are always sirens stretching and contracting in the distance, loud and rattling.

   We pushed through the light Friday crowds, walked over the bridge where there was a tramp eating a McDonald's and several Rastafarians offering to wrap my hair in thread and we turned left into the path of cart shops lining the street looking down over the dirty canal. I leant over the chipped paint railings of the bridge and watched the thick water stream past, carrying Coke cans and a legion of cigarette butts. We passed Dad's shop, the lights were all off and there were no banging metal noises vibrating out of the workroom round the back where Dad fiddled with his beloved antique guns. Through the window I saw the messy inside, still filled with its military mementos and the full of ornate, fat, painted umbrella vases.

We stood outside for a few moments, Jackson perched on a little rim of crumbing wall and me staring inside until I heard someone shout something down from above. I stared up at the landlord, who was leaning out of the red-bricked building like a melting gargoyle. The light was coming from behind him so I couldn't see him very clearly.

'Get your bloody father to phone me,' he shouted down.

I was about to answer that Dad had gone away, but the landlord had popped back inside the window, which was closed again as if he'd never leant his hooked nose out of it. I looked at Jackson nervously and shrugged. Then he took my hand and we walked home through the tumbling streets.

'Mum and Dad have gone away for a while,' I said to Jackson as I put my key in the house door and opened it.

'Where?' Jackson asked in his slow, sandy voice and we both paused in the hallway because we could hear somebody in the kitchen.

'I thought Rocco was in the pub tonight,' Jackson said.

'I thought he was,' I replied and walked into the kitchen to find a woman drinking tea and reading the paper at our kitchen table. I didn't think that I'd ever met her before. She was an energetic-looking old woman wearing a big jumper and a salmon coloured skirt. She had rings on her wrinkled fingers and red lipstick on her lips.

'Hello?' I said, alarmed.

'Oh hello,' she replied, closing the paper and looking at me and Jackson quizzically. 'My name is Mrs Arnold,' she said, and put out her hand to shake mine and then Jackson's. 'Sorry to drop in unannounced. I just thought I'd come to see if you two were getting on all right, not getting into mischief. Your mother gave me a key.' She shook her fat ball of keys, which looked as though she could quite possibly have a key to every house in London. 'I live in the next street – we've met, haven't we?' the woman said.

'I don't think so. This isn't my brother,' I said, pointing at Jackson. 'Rocco's at work. Thank you very much for coming, but there's really no need. Rocco and I can look after ourselves.'

'Yes,' the woman said. 'But your mother insisted I came, so I thought I'd just check you were fine. Do you need anything?'

'No thanks,' I said, 'you really don't have to come

round. Mum left your telephone number so we'll phone you if we have any problems, but we won't. She'll be back any day now.'

'Good. Do phone if you need anything, I'd hate to let your mother down. She's such a lovely woman.'

'Of course,' I said quickly.

'I'll be going then. Get some shopping done, you know,' she said as she swung her large fake leather handbag over her shoulder and left the house. I wondered how long Mum and Dad were planning to be gone for.

—ᴠᴠ—

VIRGIN

For unexplainable reasons I lost my virginity to Jackson that night, just one day after Mum left. By the time Rocco came home Jackson was gone and I was sitting on my bed reading, wearing pyjamas. Rocco stood in the doorway and looked at me curiously.

'You look flushed,' he said, lighting up a cigarette and stepping outside the window onto the little metal balcony attached to our house. Rocco picked up an empty glass that had been left outside and poured the dirty rainwater out so that it splashed on to the pavement while I folded over the page of my book, putting on a jumper and followed him out of the window. I looked at the angular Camden back streets that nudged and met like a hamster maze and at the back of the supermarket, which had that horrible vacant look of a place that should be full of people, eerie in the shadows bouncing off the surrounding buildings. I sat up on the rail of the balcony that night like I always did, leaning on the bit of chimney that jutted out of the wall. My legs rested open, one on the front rail and the other on the ledge.

'I'm just hot,' I lied. I hadn't planned to sleep with Jackson, but the liquid metal feeling between my legs had taken me by surprise. I didn't feel like talking about it to Rocco; it wasn't that I was ashamed, but just that every first time needs a little while to digest and diffuse around your body like a vitamin capsule. In a way I just wanted to check that sex hadn't released some vile surge of chemicals that would rust me instantly into an adult like Mum. I suppose I was also a little embarrassed.

I had gone upstairs with Jackson a couple of hours after getting home from school, and I'd closed the window. Jackson had grinned, his eyes dilated and his limbs all moving at the same time. He plugged in a little portable heater we had under the table, freeing a gust of boiling air from the plastic grates and he stood in front of it for a moment, pretending it was a fire and doing over the top actions that made me smile. I didn't plan to sleep with him. I really, really, didn't plan to sleep with him. He smelt of cigarettes and deodorant.

I smiled at his boyish face and his hands began tapping quickly over mine. Tap, tap, tap, tap, tap, tap.

It began to get hot in the loft as the coldness melted and Jackson looked around for something to occupy his hands, which wouldn't stop tapping and fidgeting. He picked up a navy blue magic marker from the dresser and began to click the top on and off, click, click, click, click, click. My skirt was crumpled against my skin, the material sticking to me. In the loft Jackson's eyes were the only cool things. I ran the corner of the duvet between my fingers thoughtfully. Jackson was wearing his shirt unbuttoned part of the way down his chest and some loose baggy trousers held up by his silver-studded belt.

'Can I draw on you with your pen?' he said, holding the pen upwards, suspended with the nib pointed towards me.

'No,' I squirmed, laughing at his seriousness.

'Come on,' he said. 'I'm holding this pen, I have to draw on something.' So I held out my hand for him to doodle on. He held my wrist, concentrating with a frown and he drew a line from the warm skin just underneath my armpit, all the way down the naked inside of my arm, over my wrist, in a circle over the palm of my hand and back down the lane of my arm to my armpit. I let my arm go limp in his grip and he kept it steady. At my armpit, I could feel the ink spilling out and mixing with my sweat, but the lines on my wrist were firm and thick. They went over the slight bumps of my veins and blurred at my palms. The ink on my

palms ran like water filling tiny dry river creases. I
watched his face as he drew, the tight lines on his
forehead made me want to put my tongue in the folds
of his frown, to make them stretch out again.

He surveyed his artwork and I wriggled up into a
kneeling position under the covers, my body feeling
hot and heavy. He drew another circle, inside the first
circle on my palm and coloured it in over and over
again so the smell of ink and blueberries filled the air
around us. I felt malleable, passive as a magician's girl
and warm as steam. Jackson held my fingers and let
the ink dry before putting his hot hand in the shadow
between my legs, his thumb pressing down on my
skin. I moved over away from the duvet cover, without
losing his hand on my leg and sat cross-legged in front
of him as he leant forward to kiss me, but I turned my
head away so his kiss touched my red cheek.

'Are you never going to sleep with me just because
it would annoy your brother?' He smiled.

I looked up at him in surprise and ran the silky
corners of the duvet through the spaces between my
fingers as he took off his shirt. I had never really
thought about it before. The heavy feeling in my body
seemed eager and strangely detached from my head.
The only thing I could compare this feeling to would
be a fever. You want liquid inside you without your
brain telling you to drink and you don't understand a
fever, although you feel it. This was the first time this

creamy feeling had been so deep and unshakable.

'Fine, I'll just draw on you,' he said. He came to lie down next to me. I was leaning back against the wall, snug as a caterpillar. Just my feet were peeking out at the end of the duvet and he took the magic marker and began on the sole of my foot, where it tickled wetly and the ink ran. Then he moved the pen up my leg, light over the soft back of my knees, curving on to the inside of my thigh and pushing back the duvet as the hot ink got higher. I didn't stop him, he pushed heavily near my knickers and I could feel the blue ink on my skin. The air around smelt of sex.

I always remember the smell of my first times, because intensity etches lovely details on to your memory. My first kiss smelt of fresh mown grass, caramels we'd been eating and Lynx deodorant. It was a very particular smell and any one of those things bring back the memory. Sex I found to have a particular smell too, like two smells mixing, sheet friction, hot saliva and the inside of underwear. He kissed me and I couldn't help but kiss back, overcome by this new ache that hit me like an injection or a cup of coffee. It took fifteen minutes.

Rocco stood right in front of me on our little balcony and looked sternly at the lines on my hands and feet, where they crawled like snail trails into my sleeves and pyjama trouser legs.

'They're very artistic doodles.' Rocco half-smiled, nodding at my arms and then, more pointedly, at my legs where you could just see the lines where they'd bled into the creases of my feet. 'Like crop circles.'

'Are you making a scene because Jackson drew on me?' I asked, looking down at the road under us. I watched Rocco's hand wrapped around the glass, which looked pretty in the light, full of smoky colour, and his skin was tense over the cool of the glass. Rocco and I used to fight properly all the time, nails and knuckles digging and biting. I stopped enjoying fighting with my brother when we got older and stronger.

At age thirteen Rocco went through six months of being sex-hyped as a rabbit, sad as a widow, bored all the time, too strong for me to inflict any physical pain on him and he had this amazing aura of tension around him. One afternoon he was being particularly horrible while we were sitting in the loft with the window open and the prickly summer polluted heat surrounding us. I couldn't think of any way to annoy him because he tended to ignore every word I said, but I had just grown a slight layer of fat under my nipples which constituted breasts, so with a rush of inspiration I took off my top. I didn't look at him, but tugged the hot material over my head as if I was simply being practical in the heat. I kept my eyes on a magazine, but sat like that right in front of him. My long hair was behind me and I could feel his eyes locked on me for ten minutes. It was hot and a drip of sweat collected between my breasts, focusing his gaze. The drip thickened and the tension grew, the smell of heat and pollution and sweat becoming overpowering in the stuffy loft, and I tried to repress smiles about this new way to torture my older brother. As the bubble of sweat fell, Rocco walked out of the loft and when he was gone I got dressed again. Afterwards I felt guilty about teasing him, but not guilty enough not to use his unbalanced hormones to taunt him whenever he annoyed me, taking off my top at the drop of a hat, but never letting him touch me.

He was annoying me now, looking at me intently on the balcony and being over protective. I had an odd desire to annoy him similarly.

'I'm hardly making a scene,' he said. 'I'm just wondering why he drew on you.' I could sense the weight and texture of his gaze on my skin, as if his eyes were blowing air on to my body. It gave me goose pimples.

'Because he felt like it,' I said. Rocco's hand tensed more around the glass and it looked fragile. I wondered if he would break it if I told him I slept with Jackson. 'He was odd and h . . .' I paused for a moment, looking at the street, running my eyes over the supermarket and the road. 'And happy,' I said. 'So he drew on me.'

'Nice. Has he drawn on you before?' Rocco asked, touching my feet lightly on the inky line running under my trousers. His touch was like touching myself, but with all the adrenalin of intimacy.

'No,' I said, watching the veins of Rocco's hands throb over the glass. 'That was the first time.'

'Ink isn't good for you,' he said oddly, watching me look up from the floor into his big green eyes.

'It's magic marker, Rocco.'

'Still ink,' he said. I smiled at Rocco and he didn't smile back, but gripped the thin glass and I felt nervous, unsure as to what he was thinking.

'Sure,' I said, phrasing my sentences carefully as if I was walking on the glass cup lightly, wondering whether it would break under my weight. 'You know what we did after he drew on me?' I focused on Rocco's knuckles whitening over the glass and then my smile stopped abruptly. Rocco squeezed the glass so hard that it snapped with a shatter under the pressure and folded in on itself in several jagged pieces that fell to the floor, covered in drips of red.

'Rocco!' I said, my eyes wide, laughing at him for acting out a filmic cliche and grabbing his wrist like he had grabbed mine, seeing the slither cuts on his fingers fill up with sticky red liquid. I looked up and Rocco wouldn't hold my gaze or look at his hand and his face was white.

'I'll get a tissue,' I said, but he grabbed me with his

uncut hand as I tried to go.

'What happened?' he said harshly. I didn't say anything, looking down at the floor of the balcony and Rocco's walking boots surrounded in shards of glass. 'What happened after he drew on you?' he said more forcefully, squeezing my arm so that it hurt.

'Let me get you a tissue, Rocco, you're bleeding,' I said loudly, trying to wriggle out of his grasp, but he wouldn't let go.

'I don't want a tissue, I want to know what happened.' He paused and I looked up at him. 'I won't let you get me a tissue until you say.'

He kept hold of me and I paused. Rocco looked young, babyish, despite his stern features and arched eyebrows. 'You know what happened,' I said, and his face froze. All the little muscles in his face were tight, his eyes wide as mine, and his grip loosened grudgingly from my wrist. I climbed into the loft from the balcony and angrily threw a packet of tissues out to Rocco for his hand. I was not laughing any more. The tissues fell to the ground but he didn't bend down to get them. He was still leaning on the balcony while I turned off all the lights and got into bed. I didn't go to sleep for ages, because of Rocco's heavy presence padding around the room, and smoking cigarettes until midnight, when he pulled down the blinds and created a thin wrinkle of streetlight through the room and got into bed.

—ɯ—

FASCINATIONS

On the Monday after Mum left I went to see Rocco at the pet shop during my lunch break, just to say hello. I went the long way round, through the back streets so that I didn't have to walk past the antique shop. The stones on the streets were wet and crumbling at the corners. I walked past a skip, which had a mattress lounging against it, all wrinkled-up like a sofa, and on top was a smashed pane of glass. The mattress was wet and the glass a heavy puddle on top. I turned right down Camden High Street and walked until I arrived at the pet shop. I stood at the entrance and looked in on the cages of hamsters sleeping in bundles on top of each other in the window display on my left. There was a huge tub of frogs near the door and on the opposite wall were rows of dank coloured fish tanks, making the room look like an occult chamber. There were goldfish, big black fish with tails like tongues and eyes like water bubbles, tropical fish, baby fish, blue, green, orange fish, all looking unhappy and cramped. There was a parrot babbling in one of the corners, and birds squawking nervously, trapped up in cages.

'You looking for anything in particular?' the man behind the desk said, toying with a novelty cat key ring.

'No thanks, my brother works upstairs,' I said.

'Oh,' he said.

I didn't like this bit of the pet shop; it smelt of torn-up toilet roll and algae from the fish tanks. Rocco worked in three smaller rooms up a very thin stone staircase, where he sold lizards, spiders and snakes. At the top of the stairs there was one of those bead curtains that clatter when you push through and then a darkened room with one frosted window at the back.

Rocco was sitting at the counter reading a book because there was no one in this bit of the shop and he looked up with a big grin when I came in, folding up his book and pushing it to the side.

This room gave me the creeps. There was a big green lizard stretched out in a long cage built into the counter, clawing languidly at the glass, its dragon chin resting on a plastic boulder. To the left of the counter there were boxes and boxes of different species of crickets, not for pets but to feed the spiders, and they made a hopeless squeaking sound. If downstairs was the commercial occult store, where mock teenage Goths went, up here was where the sinister stuff happened. I thought that the lizards and snakes could be spellbound people living out curses in the scaly, dignified bodies of reptiles behind dusty glass. In the other two rooms the walls were almost entirely made of glass tanks, packed full of curled up snakes or achingly still spindly spiders.

'How's your day going?' I said to Rocco, and leant on the counter, picking up a leaflet called 'My First Tarantula'. I didn't come to the shop much, it made me oddly nervous because it was so dark and wet. It felt morbid, full of trapped life and stale breath. I watched Rocco, there were grainy scabs on his hand from the glass. I wrapped hair around my finger and tried to smile. I didn't want him to be angry.

'Uneventful,' Rocco said. 'The usual, sold a couple of spiders, someone came in looking for a lizard for his son, nothing interesting. You?'

'Finding it difficult to concentrate.' I turned to face my brother. 'It's dumb, but I can't stop thinking about Dad.'

'That's what sex does,' Rocco smiled. 'Turns your brain to mush.'

I looked the other way, at a baby frog.

'I said I was thinking about Dad.'

'Why were you thinking about Dad?' Rocco asked.

'Because he's ill,' I snapped and Rocco shrugged.

'Dad can look after himself.'

'Sure, that's why Mum does everything for him,' I said, agitated.

'Then worry about Mum,' he replied.

'Don't be so antagonistic,' I said, moving away from the counter and causing the lizard underneath to quiver slightly. I walked briskly over to the tank of frogs and crouched down to look at their slug-fat bodies.

'Hey, Izzie,' Rocco said, looking at me with his big green eyes the same colours as the frogs'. 'It's nothing. Dad's always been kind of ill, don't worry about it.'

Before Dad began to get his spells of flu, before our parents turned into anxious, jumpy people, Rocco and I, as I've said, used to spend a lot of time in Dad's antique shop, encased in the smell of pounded metal, sawdust and gunpowder oil. We went there most Sundays until Mum found us playing with the guns and got angry. She was particularly concerned that we didn't touch the most valuable ones.

On the last Sunday we spent in the shop I was eight, and wearing a floral rose coloured dress. I had two green clips in my long red hair and red buckled shoes over white ankle socks. Rocco, aged ten, was playing with his glow-in-the-dark laces on his new trainers, his whole body lithe before adolescence tightened his joints. We were both sitting on the wooden counter.

Dad, in a desperate effort to amuse us, was dis-
assembling old guns and talking about gun history. He
wasn't remotely interested in the other antiques, the
beautiful pounded copper plates, the broken cabinet,
or the big lockable boxes. Over years and years of
trying to amuse his children Dad had shown us all
sorts of things to do with guns. He'd shown us how to
put firing pins back in old guns so they worked again,
he let us pack gunpowder, and taught us how to
choose bullets for different aged guns. Dad was
playing with a pretty, rounded rifle with a deep
mahogany handle and a real silver frame, stroking it
adoringly as though it were a cat.

'The origin of the word gun,' Dad was saying, 'may
be derived from the old middle English girl's name
Gunnilde or Gunhilda. Originally they thought it
came from Latin, but it's much more likely to be a
girl's name.' Rocco was still playing with his laces and
I had the wide-eyed vacant look that I preserved solely
for being polite to my daddy. It consisted of trying to
keep my eyes as wide as possible and keeping my
mouth in a smile. I loved the feeling of a gun in my
hand, not because I was at all enthusiastic about
killing, but because it felt very heavy and safe. All of
Dad's guns tended to be over-oiled and he fixed them
himself. They were greasy to the touch, and if you ran
your fingers over the ones with embossed metallic
patterns they felt smooth and oddly comforting.

My favourite gun was a 5-shot Colt pocket revolver. It was cased in an old rosewood and blue velvet case with different sections like a spice box and each bit fitted into the wooden box perfectly. There was a powder flask, a steel bullet mould stamped with 'Colts Patent' and a combination nipple key and turn screw, used for inserting the bullets. It had a walnut grip and an over-shined, dimpled metal body that Rocco ran a finger over while I held it. It was cold in the shop and I shivered with the ice metal frame of the gun between my fat little fingers.

'This finds support in the suggestion that in Old Norwegian "gunne" and "hilde" both mean "war".'

Rocco looked up and smiled unemotionally. 'Who would call their kid War War?' Rocco said, and Dad didn't answer. I laughed, watching him.

Rocco stopped playing with his shoelace and picked up a heavy gun from the counter.

'That's an 1875 choke-boring rifle,' Dad said.

'Don't you have something to fix?' Rocco said rudely. Usually Dad either went out and left us alone in the shop or he spent the day fixing stuff and talking on the phone in his office. He spent a lot of time organising for antiques to be shipped over from some contacts he had. Hardly anybody ever came into the shop and Rocco and I would have a lovely time playing games about wars and princesses and soldiers. I think Dad was waiting for Mum to come round, so he wasn't working in the back and it was annoying Rocco and me, who had been in the middle of a game last Sunday which we were eager to continue.

Mum came in just as I picked up a little gun from a shelf and pointed it at Rocco with an excited giggle.

'Bang, bang, bang,' I said, and Rocco died theatrically over the counter. Mum silently watched Rocco wheeze and me cackle like the Wicked Witch of the West. Rocco writhed, half-giggling and half mock-groaning on the floor. His legs convulsed into a foetal position and his neck strained backwards uncomfortably with an open mouth. I blew the tip of my gun, pretending to be a cowgirl and then Mum coughed to get our attention, so we all turned around. Dad looked scared of Mum, as if he were trying to become one of the thin old guns or fragile antique bowls and accommodate himself into their history. His eyes were hooded over like mysterious women, all sulky and tired. He had bags under his eyes and a tight mouth.

'Um, they're just playing.' Dad ventured. Mum was wearing a yellow dress and she looked pretty as the sun. Rocco and I chirped hello to her and she smiled blankly back.

'We have customers,' she said.

Rocco and I slipped through the back of the shop and into Dad's workroom where we sat opposite each other in silence, immersed in the stiff smell of pounded metal, sawdust, gunpowder and oil. We played quietly with a gun that Dad was fixing while Mum and Dad shouted at each other for an hour. These arguments always occurred in the aftermath, or were the credits for particularly loud or violent sex, which we had listened to the night before as if it was the musical equivalent of a horror film, horrible, but somehow compelling.

'I guess I should go back to school,' I said, turning to face Rocco again over the pet shop counter and half-smiling wearily.

'I guess,' he said.

'Do you remember when we used to spend every Sunday in Dad's shop?' I asked Rocco, who was feeding a lizard and he nodded. 'I liked that,' I said.

'I don't remember liking it much, Dad never took any notice of us.'

'We didn't want to have notice taken of us,' I said. 'And anyway, sometimes he was really sweet. We only remember him negatively because he became sort of negative as we got older. He used to be interesting.'

'You remember things in much rosier colours than I do,' he said, and then a woman came into the shop, looking for stick insects and Rocco had to go and look after her. I busied myself with talking to the dragon under the counter, whom I had named Puff the first time I'd come to see Rocco at the shop. Puff looked at me as if he were terribly sleepy and he curled up his tail. When I first came here the whole place had been much muskier, but Rocco kept it relatively clean although I don't know how he could stand the smell and the annoying cricket sounds for hours and hours every day. I shouted good-bye to Rocco and arrived late for my chemistry lesson.

9

—ᘯ—

SNOW

A week after Mum left it started to snow and when I woke up on Sunday to the sound of the doorbell, the blinds were open and light was shining through, making sea-slug patterns mirroring the shadows in the sky. I pulled my duvet, which had slipped down to my tummy, back up to my chin and scrunched my eyes up in a vain attempt to block out the light and the noise of the bell. Rocco heaved himself out of bed to the loft door, stepping on the soldiers and swearing sleepily. They weren't an army that morning, but some sort of struggling camp of casualties. I squinted up at him and couldn't help smiling as he hopped out of the loft. He was wearing stripy boxer shorts and his thick black hair was all messy around his face.

The room smelt of morning-sleep sweat and the

light was strange because of the snow. I carefully spun my legs from under the duvet on to the carpet, putting on Dad's cashmere jumper so you could just see my little white shorts under the soft material and then my long thin white legs. My feet at the bottom of my legs looked small and the red nail polish was chipping. I couldn't tell what time it was, but as I looked out of the window I saw the snow and smiled. It looked from our window like sea foam from broken waves and it had collected in dust piles on the naked branches of the London plane trees and made a pinafore on the steel railings. The snow looked sweaty in the creases of the pavement while the sky was super neon blue.

The weird thing about sleep is that it disorientates your sense of time, so the man at the door could have rung the bell every ten minutes or every thirty seconds, but I got the feeling he was being impatient. I followed Rocco down and perched on the bottom stair while he lit a cigarette and then opened the door to Dad's landlord from the shop, who was still wearing the wiry glasses on his big hooked nose and was holding rolled up papers in his right hand. His left hand was poised, ready to ring the bell again and he was frowning impatiently with little lines injecting into the creases of his lips. His face seemed to be dripping, especially his nose, which cascaded down over his mouth. I imagined that he was an ogre in a fairy story, trying to poison our castle with looks from his saggy eyes.

'How can I help you?' Rocco said, leaning on the doorframe and drawing woozily on his cigarette. The landlord looked Rocco up and down expressionlessly.

'Hello again,' the man said slowly, half-glancing at the thin watch on his wrist as I felt my first nervous shiver. Now that I had time to look at him properly, with his huge shadow scars around crumpled brown eyes, hooded by fat eyelids, I noticed just how ugly he was. 'Your father never phoned me,' the man said. 'Could you get him for me please?'

'I'm afraid he's not around,' Rocco said. 'He's gone away. You could leave your number and I'll get him to give you a buzz when he gets home.'

'He hasn't paid the rent in months and I need the money today, now,' the man said sharply and Rocco looked surprised before shrugging his naked shoulders apologetically. The man pushed on, asking, 'Do you know where we can find him?'

'I'm sorry, but he didn't leave an address.'

'I see,' the ugly landlord snapped. 'He owes me quite a sum, which I need. I've given that man enough slack, I need the money now.'

'There's nothing we can do about that,' Rocco said. 'He didn't leave us any money at all.'

'I could go to court about this,' the landlord said, wiping his glasses with his sleeve. I began to twitch my cold bare feet nervously over each other and chewed one of my nails.

'Sorry,' Rocco said and the man turned on his heel.

Rocco slammed the door on the landlord, making the house tremble. The hallway felt cold now because of the snowy wind and I was suddenly wide-awake. I followed Rocco into the kitchen. Without Mum around to clean, the rooms were getting quite messy. I wondered why she hadn't even phoned. Rocco hazardously pushed aside the unbalanced debris of stuff cluttering the kitchen table. He got out two cereal bowls and poured cornflakes, but we didn't seem to have any milk so we sat opposite each other picking at the dry flakes without much enthusiasm. I liked the idea of snow – it gave London a funny atmosphere.

'Snow,' I said, nodding out of the window and placing a cornflake on the tip of my tongue thoughtfully.

'Yeah, it's been ages since it snowed,' he said.

We put the radio on and the weather man advised about ice conditions on the road and traffic at Clapham Junction so neither of us spoke.

'What do you think the man's going to do?' I asked.

'I don't know.' Rocco curled his mouth into a frown. The cornflakes were becoming boring and I got up to look in the fridge, but all we had was the foul-smelling remains of a Chinese takeaway, so I closed it in disgust. I turned around and looked at Rocco, still methodically eating his dry cereal.

There was a little spider in the corner of our kitchen, so tiny and elegant that it was almost invisible. I remember one night during our family holiday in Malta, Rocco and I snuck out of the hotel and followed the sea down to the village centre where we wandered about a bit like two silent flies, watching people eat dinner on terraces over the water. Rocco and I have never been fond of large groups and it seemed lovely to be able to observe them like a theatre. We stood just at the corner of these pavement cafes, lit by glow worm lights and nobody noticed our small hovering bodies. We saw shadows more than people, not noticing features, but only floating limbs as if each person was an ant on a farm we were studying for social patterns. The worker ants rushed from table cluster to table cluster, boy and girl feet linked ritualistically under the tables, young girls tucked their hair behind their ears and sat up straight, as taut as puppets, while they flirted.

Rocco took a big plastic bag of old bread rolls from the back entrance of a restaurant and we had a fight down on the rocks near the sea. Below where the row of cafes were, we threw them at each other like ammunition and with one particularly vicious throw I toppled Rocco right off a rock and into the sea. He seemed to pause in mid-air with cartoon slowness, his hands everywhere and his legs split like a starfish. He shouted, and fell with a big splash that made me laugh. Swift as a moth I took off all my clothes and stood with my hands on my hips above him for a few moments before slipping happily into the sea with him. The water was freezing cold and sharp all over our skin, black as marsh water but scattered with the reflections of lamps and table candles. We imagined we were invisible and that our little bodies might be swept out to sea without anyone noticing, because nobody could see us under the sheets of shadows. Only insects and children are allowed to be invisible.

On our last night in tired, hot Malta, Dad had to go to hospital after 'slipping on a damp rock'. Rocco and I were sitting on our suitcases playing noughts and crosses in pen scars up our arms, just round a corner from the hotel entrance. They didn't know we were there, so we were invisible then too. We heard Mum laughing with one of the receptionists when Dad came into the hallway with a broken leg and a bandage taped scrappily to his forehead.

'What a disreputable man,' she said to the receptionist while looking teasingly at our father who sat down abruptly on the sofa. The Spanish lady giggled nervously.

'He got drunk,' Mum announced. Rocco and I continued to play as we listened, but we looked up every so often to see our disorientated father try to scratch his broken leg under the pale cast. He was more padded out at this early stage and he looked sheepish and absurd, staring dolefully at his broken leg.

'Poor darling,' Mum said, sitting down beside him and putting her arm over his hunched shoulders. 'Are you all right? Tell me exactly what happened. You hardly said anything on the phone.'

'I had a few too many,' he said, and we watched our mother try to repress her smiles, taking his damp hand in her manicured one and playing with his fingers. 'And I slipped on one of the fucking rocks,' he continued. 'I passed out.'

'Oh, I'm so sorry,' Mum said, looking worried now. 'I should have come to the hospital,' she mumbled. 'But you did tell me not to. I bet the hospital was shabby.'

'Vile,' Dad said dryly. Rocco and I stopped our game to peer around the corner, but our parents had begun to talk very quietly so that we couldn't work out what they were saying. They both looked shiny skinned, sitting on the mushroom coloured sofa in the steamy air. The walls framing them were a hazy blue colour, mottled in places by rising damp and patterned by lightning-bolt cracks running down from the ceiling. We watched Mum touch Dad's face through the heat, stroking her fingers sadly over his bandage and then down to his heavy cheeks.

I got off my suitcase and walked round so that Mum and Dad could see me.

'You OK Dad?' I asked.

'Your poor father slipped on the beach and broke his leg,' Mum said. 'So you're going to have to be very good and helpful.' She gestured to his plaster cast. Would you like to sign it?' she asked, smiling at us, and we looked at Dad for approval. He nodded dully, so I drew a badly proportioned row of kisses and wrote 'get well soon' in fat letters, but Rocco just wrote his name messily in a vertical column of uppercase letters.

I looked out of the kitchen window at dirty Camden, feeling the quietness of our evacuated house. 'What would you do if you were invisible?' I asked Rocco. From the windows of our house the snow seemed to be softening the London landscape.

'Girls' shower rooms, no contest,' Rocco smiled. 'Then I would go and sit in other people's houses, just to see what it's like.' I remembered an old black and white movie called *The Invisible Man* where they had covered the man's face in bandages so he looked like a mummy.

'I suppose you would be invisible, in a way, if you were robbing someone's house because nobody would see you. You'd slip in and out like a mosquito, drawing that bit of someone's possessions with you.'

'It would be interesting robbing someone,' he said and we both watched the little spider in the corner of the room as it spun a web around itself to put its egg sac in.

There was one pretty thing Mum and Dad owned, one thing that Rocco and I had coveted. It was a round ball of amber with an ancient bee stuck inside, clawing its way out through the honey glow. The little bee would have smelt a scent thousands of years ago, the smell of pure pollen, and excitedly crawled on to the sap tree and into the glue. Its feet wouldn't have been able to release themselves and as the sticky resin oozed over its body it would have suffocated, contentedly on a sugar high.

The bubble of yellow was sitting in the middle of the kitchen table and I picked it up distractedly and spun it around my hand, the orange stone so shiny that it almost felt wet. Insects see much less than humans so the bee wouldn't have been able to see the sap. They survive on the odours and vibrations that are everywhere around them, but that humans can't sense. Ants lay down a chemical trail and constantly touch each other to pass on messages. Female moths send out thick sex chemicals. I thought I could still smell the landlord in the house, hot stale breathy smells trying to ferment the new bottleneck mess of our house.

Rocco looked agitated. The curl of his frown was

tight and his eyes were looking sideways out to the window, where Dad's landlord was talking on his mobile phone. The kitchen table was covered in ugly stuff, wrinkled paper, unopened letters. I closed my eyes and put my hands over the curve of my eyelids, pressing lightly at the creases and then opening them on to my brother's brow. Rocco didn't take his eyes off the man outside.

'Was that the first time you slept with Jackson?' Rocco said suddenly. I looked at my brother's profile without him returning the gaze. His big hands were steady as sleeping mice folded over each other on top of the debris, and mine were restless.

'Yeah,' I said submissively and he turned towards me with a slight smile. He raised his eyebrows a little and looked mockingly at me.

'Was it nice?' he said. 'I'm sorry I acted stupid. I want to know now, did you enjoy it?' he still had cuts on his fingers from the broken glass.

I felt I was walking into something. His innocent eyes were glinting and he looked like he used to look when he was younger and would wind circles around me, making me talk about things that made me nervous. I was small inside his gaze, important yet tiny. A huge force focussed on a pinprick, intentionally burning me up. Rocco is quiet around people, but more out of habit than shyness. If he wanted to, he could give a perfect flow of easy conversation and make you feel as if you were being interesting. He had made me describe each kiss I'd ever had to him, slowly, in calm detail. I could never do anything without telling him about each aspect, each taste. I don't think there will be any surprises for him when he reads this catalogue of first times as he already seems to have been keeping good track of my innocence. I'm not writing this for him, I'm writing it so I can stop feeling so guilty.

'Yes,' I said, and his eyes softened around the dilating pupils.

'On your bed or mine?' he asked.

'Mine,' I allowed. 'Of course mine,' I said, smiling without thinking and Rocco looked up at me. I felt a jab in my throat and energy cut up into my brain. The man outside was pacing beside the wall, the house smelt cold.

'What did he say to persuade you?' Rocco asked.

'Nothing,' I said tightly, embarrassed that he assumed I could be persuaded with a line. 'I wanted to,' I said.

Rocco blushed and I felt oddly pleased that he had begun the game and I was instantly winning. It served him right and if he wanted to know I'd tell him. His hands even began to fidget, waking up and fiddling with the damp corners of the newspapers lining the table.

'I guess that I didn't want to sleep with him at first.

I wasn't wearing a bra,' I added. 'Also, I was nervous that you'd walk in, but he laughed at me. He drew all up my arm and I got wet, so I wanted to sleep with him, only I was scared you'd walk in and get angry.'

'I wouldn't have got angry,' Rocco lied, and I grinned at my brother, who looked so childish and serious sitting opposite me at the long kitchen table with his bowl of cornflakes. 'Or maybe just a little,' he said, letting himself smile.

'But then he drew up my thigh, tickling the back of my knee and then the inside of my leg up to the edge of my knickers. I didn't think he'd have the nerve to keep drawing all the way up and once he was up there I didn't have the heart to push him down again. He pressed on my skin with his finger and dropped the pen.'

'Were you thinking straight?' Rocco asked.

'Of course I was,' I snapped, lying. 'I wanted to sleep with him, I had this lovely cream feeling in my body instead of blood. I suppose I was clouded by it, but you have to have that change or you'd never want somebody's ugly body part anywhere inside you. I really wanted . . .' I trailed off slightly, thinking it had gone too far, I didn't want to push Rocco. His brow was creased and his eyes dilated. I hated it when Rocco looked like Dad. I moved my hair over to one side of my shoulder and Rocco looked at the man on the phone outside again.

'And?' Rocco prompted. I raised my eyebrows.

'He kissed me up against the wall,' I said carefully, feeling nervous and forced. 'He wasn't sweet about it, I suppose that was the problem. Of course I didn't really know how it was meant to happen. He didn't make me do anything disgusting; but, I don't know, he wasn't nice.'

'I could kill him,' Rocco said.

'Don't be angry,' I said, putting my hands over his tense fingers and feeling ashamed. His eyes were flashing and I had to move each finger in turn because they were tight as wood. The words made my actions horribly documented and definite and although I wove my hand into his, for a second I hated him for making me talk about it.

'Sorry,' I said, amazed that I was apologising. 'I didn't mean to tell you all that.' I felt bad because he wasn't moving, locked in position like a puppet. I hated not understanding my brother. His whole body was tense, even his eyes looked like they'd turned into marble circles cold as the house, yet moist as the amber in my hand. I noted that his hands were sweating and mine were too. I wanted to tell him how much it hurt and for him to hug me, as if I'd grazed my knee. Only to say the words 'it hurt' would have been too graphic and too visual. When we were little I used to quantify how much I loved him and he'd say it back. 'I love you more than Mum and Dad put together', I'd say. 'I love you more than chocolate,' he'd say, giving me a kiss.

Rocco was never pretty. I was the pretty one with my white skin and long hair, he was the beautiful one because while my big eyes fitted my face, his stood out as huge. His cheekbones were too defined, his eyebrows too thick, his dress sense messy as if everything was slipping off him. He caught the attention of men and women alike, but never showed any interest in boys. He always liked girls a lot, especially blonde girls, and they liked his brooding presence and quiet thoughtfulness. Unlike Mum, the young girls liked the way he made them feel uncomfortable with his silence or his sex-laced comments.

I used to watch him with his girlfriends and never once did I see one who didn't look nervous and ready to fight. He was so steady that perhaps other people simply looked giddy in comparison. He wasn't in love with any of them and he didn't lie to them, but somehow they all thought that he'd come round eventually. He never did and the girls would leave him, either sad or angry and he'd let them leave without flinching. He had a strange melancholy analogy of affairs being like war. You met and added up the weapons. The boy moved forward, the girl perhaps let him, one point to him, one potentially for her. He phones her, they arrange some sort of battleground, they create a treaty. They prolong each battle, fighting subtlety with conversation for the upper hand until full on war breaks out one night in the dark when they have sex. There is no perfect union, because a perfect union would be lukewarm water. He took me to see Rodin's sculpture 'The Kiss' once and pointed out each muscle with the certainty of a doctor, persuading me that the lover was pushing the girl away, not drawing her close. I hated this idea. Rocco quoted Byron, 'a mind at peace with all below, A heart whose love is innocent!' and then he looked sombre, his dark eyes wide, and said that there simply was no such thing as an innocent lover. When he said that I laughed, but nervously. This idea of continual, heated tension for the rest of life made me feverish. I didn't want to be like Mum and Dad.

When we were little Rocco would kiss me on the lips sometimes, practising for kissing other girls. I'd be sitting on the edge of the balcony, leaning back on the chimney and he'd stand between my legs. When the guns in Dad's shop were given characters they often kissed, because they had such dramatic pouting mouths. We were playing out on the balcony with the two old guns kept in the house. Rocco was holding the more male gun with a black-inked hard wood frame and a dark metal pipe. It didn't have any frills or embossed metal ribbing, while mine was almost entirely shiny silver. It had bits of ivory and the metal latch came far away from the frame of the gun in a twisting pattern. Rocco's gun had just been called into battle, fighting goblins in Brazil and my gun wasn't going to see his for a long while. So our guns clasped their cold expressionless mouths together for a moment, before Rocco' s gun fell down by his side. I looked at him accusingly, annoyed that he had broken the moody bubble of our game.

'It's just that they're dead, they don't have any blood,' Rocco said, and I was shocked. Perhaps to adults inanimate objects might be dead, but in my childish head my guns were very much alive.

'You know what I mean,' Rocco said. 'They can't bleed and they can't really kiss. They can't even shoot. They're dead.'

What compelled Rocco about blood was that it was a fluid and it rushed around inside us keeping us alive, yet we associate it with death. The soldiers, who were dead, didn't have any blood. The guns didn't have any blood. But Rocco and I did have blood and it rushed to my lips when as a child he kissed me, even though it wasn't like a proper kiss. His rough lips touched mine only for a prolonged moment. Then, like a nervous snake, his hot tongue climbed down into my mouth and I couldn't help myself from starting to laugh. He stopped and looked upset as I tried to stop laughing, but what he did seemed so funny. I was only ten and he was only twelve. He kissed me again for practice a year later and all I could think about were the sticks Dad stuck into the antique guns, which gave them the power to shoot. That time I didn't laugh, it was just interesting in the way broken pots, fire and dead moths were interesting.

—᙭—

10

CIGARETTES

Even by this time, in the first couple of weeks, I know
now that Rocco had found something to explain Mum
and Dad's behaviour, but he didn't tell me about it
then. I expect I would have done the same thing if I'd
found it, dropped it in an empty cereal carton and
stuffed the whole thing in the bin, pretending I never
saw it. At this point I was still under an illusion of
normality. Dad was tired, he kept getting flu, so they
went on holiday. I suppose Rocco understood the
world better than me and could tell the normal from
the odd. Rocco told me about this early discovery
many months afterwards, when he was trying to make
amends for all that he later did. When he told me, I
didn't have the energy to allow all of London's
turbulence and friction to resurface in my head. I
hardly even nodded when he spoke of what he'd

found, hardly even frowned, lying on our bed in Paris where we moved.

On Wednesday there was a fuzzy message from Mum on the answering machine. It seemed to suggest that there was nothing to worry about and that the landlord was taking care of everything. We wondered what was being taken care of exactly, but there was no contact number to follow up. Jackson came over that morning and we both bunked school, pretending we couldn't get there because of the snow. For a while we sat in the slowly disintegrating kitchen, cluttered in the way only two teenagers left alone could make a kitchen. Jackson looked disgusted by the state of it. The floor to the left of the fridge was sticky from 7-up and the place smelt of Chinese food. The old autumn leaves and the melting snow were mixed into sludge, which was clogging up our drains and making the steps outside the house slippery. Mum's plant in the sitting room, which grew out of a heavy, blue glazed pot, was dying because neither Rocco nor I had any desire to keep the silly thing alive, as were the plants in the kitchen. I had knocked down the multi-coloured plant in the hall by mistake and the pot was split down the middle, bleeding dirt. It looked like a dry spider that had suffocated behind a curtain in high summer, its tentacles splayed out helplessly, dry as wire. Dead leaves were scattered sadly on the floor like crepe paper. There was mouldy fruit giving off a faintly acidic smell from the fruit bowl and two of the seven little lights in the hallway had blown.

Jackson dressed messily and cheaply, but he was actually quite neat. He always folded up his shirts and he hated ash on his bedroom carpet, so he looked uncomfortable in the chaos of the kitchen. I was still in my pyjamas.

Rocco opened Mum and Dad's post, which was full of boring bills and leaflets. Mum got a lot of animal rights leaflets, refugee centres demanding money, invitations to protest marches she always meant to go to, but never did. Dad got more substantial post, antique catalogues, shipment details, party invitations and bills. One bill said that Dad hadn't paid the gas after the third warning so they were cutting it off. They said that the gas would be removed temporarily at eight o'clock that night and they would shut off the mains if there was still no payment within a week. I laughed sadly at the sight of the horrible bill, angry that Mum and Dad had forgotten to pay it.

'Where exactly are your parents?' Jackson asked disdainfully, lighting up a cigarette while I tried hard to stop laughing by holding the edge of the table and tensing my breath into deep, almost regular breathing. It was obviously nervous laughter, and gave me the distinct feeling that my head was floating off my neck. When the giggles subsided I got up to make myself some toast, but it turned out that all the bread was mouldy. I had an odd feeling of being surveyed or on display like a mounted insect, but I ignored it.

'They've gone away,' Rocco said. 'We aren't actually sure where, they've been acting a bit odd.' He shrugged.

'What are you doing for money?' Jackson asked.

'Running out of it,' Rocco said.

'Aren't you going to work today?' Jackson asked Rocco.

'I cancelled,' my brother said. 'I thought you two might get bored without me to amuse you.' He raised his eyebrows and smiled at Jackson, who glanced absently at his cigarette.

'That was very thoughtful,' Jackson mumbled sarcastically.

'Stop it,' I laughed. 'I don't need either of you to baby-sit me.'

'She used to need me to baby-sit her,' Rocco said to Jackson. 'She used to be always grazing her knees and cutting her fingers.'

'Lot of use you were, you fainted at the sight of blood,' I said and Jackson laughed.

'This place is a tip,' Jackson said, looking around at our mess.

'It is a bit,' I said. 'You want to clean it up?'

'No thanks,' he said, standing up. 'It's not my mess. Shall we go upstairs?'

*

Up in the loft all the soldiers and the two antique guns were lying on the floor along with a collection of dirty coffee cups. There was a pattern of cigarette-burns on the paintwork to the right of Rocco's bed, and some on the carpets. The whole room was very bright, the blue light reflecting off the snow down on the streets. Jackson looked nervous, his eyes continually reverting to the antique guns on the floor as we all sat down. He had seen the guns a hundred times before in the living room, but perhaps he was shifty about them now because they were in the middle of our room, surrounded by the tin army. One gun was propped up on a small hill of soldier bodies, as if the bodies were a trench and the other looked dead, strewn on the floor. Jackson sat on my unmade bed and began to roll a spliff on his knee, the paper crumpling awkwardly under his heavy fingers. It was about eleven in the morning and as the room began to fill with sweet-smelling smoke I got up and turned my back to the wall, slipping off my pyjama top and putting on a normal T-shirt, exposing my bare back and the curve of my breast for a moment in the process, but I left my shorts on.

After I was dressed I picked up one of the guns from the floor and threw it up in the air, letting the pipe spin around its own leg twice and fall solidly back into my hand. I threw it so the tip only just missed smashing against the ceiling and Jackson watched the gun spin up and tumble down again. Then Rocco and I began to play catch with it, throwing it back and forth in a smooth arch between us.

'Where did you get the soldiers?' Jackson asked.

'Dad's shop,' Rocco answered.

'Does the gun work?' Jackson asked, his throat dry and his eyes moist with watching. Rocco and I shook our heads simultaneously and while we threw the gun back and forward I thought how self-righteous Jackson looked, smoking and watching. He knew the gun was full of cement and couldn't shoot because he'd asked before.

I caught the gun and placed it carefully on the floor, picking up the other one while watching Jackson, and feeling its hard cold metal handle under my skin. I laughed when I glanced up at Jackson's tight features. His mouth pursed into a bow and his blue eyes squinting at me. I put the gun down and smiled at Rocco, who had lain down backwards on his bed with a grin. Since I'd slept with Jackson, Rocco hadn't liked him and Jackson knew it. They were tense with each other and their faces amused me. I hate thinking about Jackson now. Trying to slot together memories of him makes me feel sick. I need to see each snapshot in isolation, because if I remembered it all at once I wouldn't believe it happened. Instead I see him as an actor playing different roles.

*

While the three of us were sitting in the loft we heard a cooing sound outside our window. It wasn't loud to begin with, it sounded a little like the smell of baking bread would. I imagined a fat pigeon with a warm phlegm-filled throat and ruffled feathers. Then there was a scrape and the cooing sound got sharper and fuller. Another colder pigeon voice began to make some noise too, not a scrape or a coo, but more of a shriek and Rocco and I looked at each other enquiringly. I put my head out of the window but couldn't see anything, so I climbed out on to the little balcony and looked around. Rocco followed me, balancing himself with his big hands while Jackson stayed inside. The noise was loud and violent to our left, rising and falling and dragging. Horrible sounds; scrapes and squirts mixed with shrieks. Then with the gusto of gladiators, two vast grey London pigeons circled into view above the chimney.

I strained my neck to see them and Rocco watched effortlessly as they puffed out their smoke-coloured feathers. They moved around each other in an odd, smooth way, but pecked randomly. Not graceful birds, pigeons, but more graceful with adrenaline than I've seen before. They had the look of moths, or some other less fluid insect and their intense candy eyes locked together. One of them, the fatter one with a black head like a cap, snapped at the smaller one and his beak dug into his neck. The smaller one cowered and almost lost balance, but somehow managed to swing its neck around underneath the other to wound its breast, taking a chunk of the big pigeon out with him, but as he did so his straw feet cluttered over the side and he landed on the tiles of the roof. He almost could have landed on top of us, but got caught in the drain above with a thud and a slosh of old rain water. I saw Jackson look vaguely out of the window, uninterested.

'Ugh,' I groaned as the big pigeon swooped down and began ruthlessly to tear up the smaller pigeon. 'This is vile,' I said, but Rocco was riveted by the spectacle: the mesmerising quality of the gore, feathers, red water and noise. His face was white, which was a sign that he was disgusted but, as I've said, disgusting things interest him. The bird was pecking and ripping while the smaller bird tried weakly to get away. The small pigeon, in a last desperate effort, squirmed to its feet but lost balance in the process. It looked aghast, face bloody and strained, eyes lopsided and then toppled over the drain and fell like a slice of steak to the ground.

The winner, suddenly alone on the London rooftop, didn't quite know what to do with itself and it looked around as if it expected some huge round of applause. Then it hobbled, disheartened, back to the chimney, its leg hurt, and Rocco slow-clapped it with interest. I turned to face him on the small balcony, leaving just a little space between us and he looked over my head at where the fight had taken place.

'Thus he died,' Rocco quoted. 'And all the life struggled out of him;

and as he died he spattered me with the dark red

and violent-driven rain of bitter-savoured blood.'

Rocco paused and I noticed how the dusky natural light brought out a severe quality in his face and his warm eyes didn't look so much like they were melting.

'What's that from?' I asked.

'Klytemnestra's speech in the Agamemnon,' he said and I looked blank. I turned away and felt annoyed. He always had to be cleverer than anyone else.

'I thought you hated blood,' I said.

'Only your blood,' he laughed, looking at me.

'Really?' I said, surprised. 'Why?'

'I don't know,' he said. 'I guess no one likes to see the thing they love being in any pain. Shows you're not perfect. Shows you're going to die.'

'Nice,' I said. We paused.

'That was beautiful,' he said, nodding up towards the drain.

Jackson was looking at us warily as if we were on a cinema screen, and when we climbed back inside I sat on his knee, but he looked in the opposite direction.

'That was disgusting,' he said.

*

We ordered pizza and, when the doorbell rang, both boys went downstairs. Jackson tried to stay upstairs with me while Rocco went down, but Rocco looked so stern that he followed. Lonely, I watched a fly buzz around the room for a few moments before lighting up one of Jackson's cigarettes.

I'd smoked about half of it and was leaning on Rocco's bed about to put it out on the metal balcony, when Rocco opened the loft door and stood looking at me. I turned around and steadily stared back.

'It's such an ugly habit,' Rocco said carefully. He was holding three glasses of water, which he put down on the floor. 'I wish you wouldn't,' he said and moved towards me while I got up from the floor and backed away. He didn't look angry, but then he never looks angry. He had that slight hardness around his eyes. The strap of my top slipped down my shoulder and I pulled it up again, still looking straight at him and taking another deep drag of my cigarette. The fly buzzed annoyingly around the room.

I remembered fighting with Rocco in the garden five years ago – the last time it snowed. I threw snow right in his face and the snowball fight progressed to all out fighting, as we tried to trip each other up with our big Wellington boots. I screamed and ran away, shuffling snow behind me as I skipped. My heart beat faster and faster as he grabbed my arm from behind, slipping his strong legs behind my little ones so that I tripped backwards, kicking wildly in the snow and laughing. I grabbed snow and stuffed it into his face while shouting for him to get off because there was snow melting freezingly in my knickers and he was hurting.

'Say that I'm the best,' he laughed and I tried to put more snow in his face while shaking my head. He knocked the snow out of my hand.

'Say it,' he said, and although he was hurting me, I couldn't help laughing. His body was heavy over mine, his knees in the snow on either side and he was digging my cheek into the stinging snow, but I refused to say it and eventually he got off.

'You look like a slut when you smoke,' Rocco said, standing in front of me in the loft. 'You also look like a slut when you undress when you know two boys are going to watch you. Jackson was almost coming in his pants.'

I raised my eyebrows. Rocco was wearing one of Dad's second-hand shirts, complete with dented cuff-links, and his hair was too long, slipping in straggly curls over his head.

'I don't do it when anyone else is around,' I said.

'Don't I count?' he said and I shrugged, kissing on the filter and feeling heady and happy. 'Put it out,' he said sternly. The air was cold around me.

'No,' I said, stepping up on to the bed with my bare

feet and standing next to the wall above my brother to the right of the window. The room was caramel thick with smoke and I moved carefully, shivering as Rocco got close.

'Put it out,' he repeated, and I took another deep breath, slightly scared.

'No, I'm not going to do it just because you say so,' I said uncomfortably, holding the cigarette out to the side and putting my long hair over my other shoulder.

The duvet was making halos softly around my feet and I stared at my brother with wide unblinking eyes. Rocco laughed and I looked serious this time. He stepped up on to the bed very close to me so that I was standing with my back to the wall. He took my wrist stiffly in his hand and squeezed it just about where the veins in my wrist were.

I saw Jackson at the door holding the pizza awkwardly and I didn't say anything, but let Rocco take the cigarette from between my tensed fingers and put it out just next to my bare foot, stamping it into his duvet and singeing the material. Rocco's face was so close to mine that I could feel his breath, his hands were hot around my waist and his eyes exactly like my own. I looked over to Jackson, who looked back stonily across at Rocco and me.

I wriggled away from my brother and smiled at Jackson, but he didn't smile back. Instead he put the pizza down on the floor and turned around, walked downstairs and out of the front door without saying anything. I felt that horrible household hush and nervous feeling in my tummy.

I looked at Rocco quizzically and he shrugged as I grabbed my jumper to go after Jackson, not bothering to put any shoes on.

'Where are you going?' Rocco asked.

'To see what's wrong,' I said and rushed down the stairs and out of the house, just in time to see Jackson turning off our road into Camden High Street.

'Hey!' I shouted after Jackson, but he didn't turn round, so I slid breathlessly through the snow after him, my feet aching as the fragile white ice crunched between my toes before my feet went numb. When I caught up with him he turned lazily to face me, his cheeks red.

'What's wrong?' I said.

'I don't think we should see each other any more,' he said expressionlessly.

I felt very cold and naked standing in front of him with my bare legs and people seemed to be staring. My hands were cold, so I ran them awkwardly through my hair before asking why in a very small voice, wriggling my bare toes into the London snow.

'It was fun, but I just don't want to see you anymore.'

'Why?' I asked again, getting angry now, and he didn't say anything, but turned away from me and started to walk towards his house. 'I slept with you,' I shouted after him, but he didn't turn around. 'Jackson! Don't just go!' I shouted, but he kept walking and after a while I began to make my way home, my feet crushing the grey ice as I moved, looking back at Jackson every so often until he turned into another road disappearing from view. I stood outside our empty house in the bright light, but a van beeped its horn at me so I stepped slowly inside, making sure I didn't slip on the wet stairs.

I always saw scars as proof of pain, and I had the idea that if every pain I felt was solidly documented in scars then I could perhaps trace the loss of innocence. I'd bled for Jackson and I wondered if I had a scar up inside me now. Rocco had a scar across his nose courtesy of a tantrum and the eight-year-old me. We had been playing tag and he tripped me over so I tumbled head first into a wall, banging my head. I screamed at him as he darted behind mum's bed and I picked up the nearest object, which happened to be one of mum's stiletto-heeled boots and I flicked my hand backwards so that all the blue veins in my wrist stuck upwards. The boot felt heavy as a piece of solid ammunition in my palm and I launched it towards my brother so that the needle heel smacked him straight between the eyes, drawing blood over the varnished floor and sheets. Other scars include the ribbon on my wrist from where I fell off the swing, shooting straight through the centre of my palm with a very fine line that distorts some of the creases. Rocco has numerous round scars on his fists from hitting things, my knees are covered in them from climbing trees, and with carpet burns from when we fought on the floor of the loft. I wondered if these were maps of innocence lost, or just that our skins scarred easily.

Before Rocco or I knew about boy/girl etiquette, he used to check me over for scars as if he was calculating my actions. He'd take off all my clothes and I'd lie down in the loft, stiff as a doll. My body was thin and tall with elbows and knees pointy like wooden joints and I closed my eyes when I lay down, just like those dolls with fluttering eyelids. He'd examine me mostly for scars, but also cuts and bruises on my doll porcelain child skin. He'd lift my arms up and check my joints, lift my light knees with two fingers and let my calf swing. He'd put a hand between my stump breasts and check my quick heart beat and then turn me carefully over and run his fingers over the bones of my snake spine to make sure it was straight. His hands would skim all the way up my back to my neck, where he'd pause under my skull with my sweaty hair covering his hands. Then his hand would scuttle like the legs of a soft spider down to the base of my spine. He'd squeeze my limbs for broken bones, look down my mouth and make my eyes follow his fingers in an oval over my face. He would count my scars, as if he was keeping track of childhood through them.

He was adamant that I should keep on being as innocent as possible for as long as possible, that I should delay my first times and make them last. However there were certain tensions in his argument. If I were as innocent as he thought he wanted me to be then he wouldn't have so much fun when I was around. As it was, his frequently lewd comments, his overt hedonism or any of the other things never shocked me. Rocco and I were always fighting, inventing scars on each other and he wouldn't like it if I was mortified by innocent shame each time he touched me or if I cowered under a rosy blush every time he swore. He wanted me to be perfectly innocent, but he'd talk to me about the different ways insects had sex or burden me with gory details from history, movies and books. Perhaps he just wanted to be the one to shape my innocence, or loss of it. I wouldn't want to avoid first times, even though it is first times that slowly syringe out your innocence.

When I got in, tears in my eyes, Rocco simply leaned over and picked up one of my tears in a ball on the top of his finger and put it in his mouth. It was like a tiny insect, round and jewelled. When Rocco was little he would scare me by finding bugs in the garden and, with quiet ritual solemnity, place the ugly half-dead creatures on the tip of his tongue while I watched in disgust. He'd keep his eyes closed as if asleep, his nose unwrinkled, and then he'd dance his tongue about before using his teeth to slide the beetle into the palm of his hand.

I wonder what insect pain felt like. I suppose that in theory they would have less capacity for pleasure in their tightly armoured little bodies and therefore less capacity for pain, but it's terribly difficult to measure pleasure and pain. There is a type of ethics called Utilitarianism that Rocco told me about once. The utilitarians claim that morality should be based on the greatest pleasure for the greatest number. The real problem they run up against is that nobody can prove that an insect splatted against a wall doesn't feel the same amount of pain as a philosopher would feel if splatted against a wall.

I suppose the first time I felt pain it was just an undeveloped tingle in the womb, like a tiny shot of electricity into my baby veins. It might even have been nice in its undeveloped form, shivering under my skin with a sensation similar to the feeling in one's lips after kissing a boy. Mum got food poisoning from oysters when she was seventeen weeks pregnant with me. You'd have thought she might have given up strange food for nine months, but she likes oysters. I think oysters gave me my first pain, and I resent this primary disillusionment. It must have been such a terrifying sensation, trapped in this wet cave being poisoned into pain by liquid you couldn't stop pumping in and out of you. When I said this to Rocco he looked at me and remarked scientifically that a baby was not aware enough to either develop a dislike for oysters or to feel trapped by the concept of pain.

A baby might not be aware of being trapped, but being knitted out of blood and gooey proteins and trapped in an underwater cave must contribute to mental instability. I began as a dumb leech, sucking on Mum's body fluids. I know that everybody began this way, but that doesn't make it any more comforting. I remember my total disgust when I found out where babies were made and where they emerged from. It was much more disturbing than sex, probably because sex wasn't compulsory, while I definitely had seen my first view of the world with my body still trapped in Mum's vagina.

Most cities are wet, dirty with their fast muddy rivers. In the future I suspect that the authorities will try to minimalise the quantity of fluid in the world, because fluid is unsanitary. Fluids are mud, oil, acid and blood. Solids are metal, wood, plastic and stone. Aids is carried in blood or semen, malaria is carried in mosquito resin, cholera in urine, bacteria thrives in mud. People simply don't catch many diseases from concrete. The world will become full of powdered milk and dry dirt. They'll have a difficult time getting rid of blood and water, the essential liquids, but at least those are partially controllable. Babies will be reared in polystyrene containers, fed on powdered calcium and protein with engineered genes, so they have nobody else's mistakes etched into them from the start. No babies will be conceived in drunken moments on the kitchen table because scientists will have eradicated semen to make sex a dry procedure, and there will be no alcohol. All liquid is ultimately made of solids anyway. There would be a factory in some suburban green-belt area called 'The Liquid Factory' where liquid would be hidden or compounded into sanitary solids. Everybody would be innocent without fluids, but it doesn't sound very nice, dry sex, dry babies, dry earth.

—〰—

11

ORANGES

Rocco says that we can't even write Mum and Dad a postcard from our new home in Paris. He is lying next to me asleep as I write, looking charmed as a baby in our hostel bed with his dark eyes closed and his big body tossing and turning, sweating against the powdery sheets. His leg is caught, wrapped around in one of the sheets, making him uncomfortable, but I won't move it because then he'll wake up. He gets so nervous when I write because he knows that I'm writing about him and what he did, but as far as I know he hasn't dared to read it. He understands that I'd leave him for good if he did, and he doesn't want to risk that again. I love him so much, more than anyone, and I've ended up giving up everything for him, but if he read this I'd have my bags packed in a second. Less than a second, because there isn't really anything to pack. I'd just take my notebooks, my passport and half of the money. But it hasn't come to that yet. We still share a room and we argue sometimes, but we don't talk about what happened and sometime soon he says we're going to move to another city and find another place to live, like two mad hatters.

Without Mum in the house, the rooms were getting messy. The first time Dad got flu, the house was the cleanest I've ever seen it. The kitchen table was blank of clutter with only the yellow placemats lined up with four chairs. There was a full bowl of fruit in the middle of the table for the entire fortnight, replenished daily with apples and kiwis and oranges. Mum liked oranges and she always peeled them in the same way, cutting them into segments first and easing off the amber coloured skin. Everything was vivid in the house, bright and cool.

'Hey Mum,' I said, coming into the clean kitchen and dumping my school bag next to the shuddering white fridge. 'How's Dad?' I took off my school jumper and tied it around my waist. I was thirteen then.

She put a carefully sliced segment of orange in her mouth and shrugged. All her hair was pinned up on her head and there were no loose bits.

'He'll be fine,' she said and smiled. She had a brilliant smile. 'Did you have a good day at school?' she asked. I looked in the very organised and full fridge, taking out some pasta salad from a labelled white container and eating it standing up, with my fingers. 'Use a fork Isabel,' she said, but I continued to stand and eat and she didn't object again.

'School was fine,' I answered.

'Where's Rocco?' she asked, wiping her sticky fingers on a white paper napkin. I shrugged because he was in detention, and at this stage she still got worried about those sorts of things so we didn't tell her if he got in trouble. Later she stopped caring as much; she didn't ask, so we didn't tell. I often wonder if they blanked out the bad things we did just as we ignored the bad things they did.

'Is Dad asleep?' I asked.

'Yeah, finally,' she said.

'What's wrong with him?' I asked.

'Flu,' she said curtly.

'Can't people get flu jabs nowadays?' I said, licking my fingers as I finished off the last piece of pasta from the tub. I remember thinking how lovely and clean the kitchen smelt. 'I'm sure I got a flu jab at school. Does that mean I can't catch it from Dad?'

'You won't catch it,' she said, 'But you shouldn't see him anyway, just in case. Those jabs don't always work.'

'But shouldn't he get the jab?'

'He's just fragile. You remember when he broke his leg in Malta?' I nodded confidingly. 'Well it turns out that he lost enough blood to have to have more blood put in him. He may have got into a fight.'

'Really?' I said. 'A fight?'

'Well I don't believe that a fall would cause these sort of effects.'

'It was ages ago.'

'I know,' she said.

I got the feeling I was annoying her now with my questions. I put the lid on the container and put it back in the fridge. There was tons of food in the fridge, big slabs of cheese, chocolate bars, celery, two chickens wrapped in clear plastic, two bottles of milk, some unopened orange juice.

'Don't put that back in the fridge if it's empty,' she laughed, wrapping the neat triangles of orange skin in the napkin and putting them in the dustbin while I took the box out of the fridge again and placed it obediently on the counter. She ran the tap over her empty plate and gave it to me to put in the dishwasher with the pasta container, but the machine was full.

'It's all clean,' I said, looking up at my mother.

'So it is,' she replied, looking quite happy and taking the things from me and arranging them next to the sink.

'I got an A in my English essay today,' I said.

'Really? What was the essay about?' she said.

'A play,' I answered.

'Could you be any more specific?' she laughed.

'*Othello*,' I said, and she looked thoughtful, trying to remember if she'd read it.

'Shakespeare,' I added, struggling through the mess in my bag to find the paper, giving it to her to look at. 'Rocco helped me,' I said.

Before Mum got all caught up in sadness, she used to keep a box devoted to Rocco and me, full of our artwork and our report cards. She did adore us, even though we weren't the perfect little children she had intended us to be. In the beginning she used to love everything, she loved the house and kept everything inside perfect, she loved the fact that she and Dad ran their own business, often saying proudly that they could take a day off to take us to the zoo or out to the country for the weekend, because they were their own bosses. She loved it when either Rocco or I did something well or said something clever and she would show things we did to Dad proudly. 'Look what good genes she must have,' I heard Mum laugh once when she sat on Dad's knee at the kitchen table and showed him a spelling test I had done well in. But above all, Dad was who she loved.

As we got older the four of us split off into them versus us. Mum and Dad had their secrets, we had ours. They argued, they made mistakes, we watched, we listened, we didn't help. Dad got ill more often, Mum would spend more time in her dressing gown and watch more television. They didn't go together to the shop so much, Mum didn't sit on his knee and read Dad the good bits of our report cards, they didn't get angry about the bad bits. After a while they hardly even read them because there was always something more dramatic going on, and by the time I was fifteen I rarely even gave them to her. She still had the box of our accomplishments and photographs in their bedroom, but she had stopped adding to it or looking at it.

'I guess I should go and do my homework now,' I said.

'Sure, have fun, don't wake up your father,' she said, and I put my school bag over one shoulder and walked upstairs. When I got to the landing I stood outside their bedroom for a moment, listening to see if Dad was awake although I couldn't hear anything inside. I listened a bit closer, with my ear right to the door, but I still couldn't hear anything except the faint rustling of the curtains and his heavy breathing. I was curious to see Dad because for the past week we hadn't been allowed in, although we'd heard arguments reverberating from under the floor of our loft. I put my bag down on the landing floor and rested my hand on the door knob for a moment before turning it, the smooth metal fitting perfectly into the palm of my hand as the door opened with an animal creak.

Inside the air was dry and dark, as if there were layers and layers of grey mosquito netting hanging from the ceiling. It smelt of marijuana and cigarette smoke even though the windows were open. My limbs felt awkward and long, standing in the doorway looking at my naked father splayed out on the bed with the sheets all crumpled to one side, his eyes closed. His skin was shiny, his hair thin on top of his head and his cheekbones shadowy against the sweaty pillow. I stood for a frozen moment staring at him and then he jumped with his eyes still closed and grabbed the pillow from under his head and threw it off the bed, making me exit the room much quicker than I had entered it, shutting the door with relief.

I leant on the door for a moment to catch my breath, feeling hot under my woollen school tights and tight blouse. I listened at the door and was reassured to hear his heavy, regular breathing through the quiet. I could hear Mum emptying the dish washer downstairs, plates clicking together as they were piled on top of each other in the cupboards. Then I heard Rocco's key in the door and his footsteps in the hallway. He said hello to Mum and when he got to the landing where I was waiting for him I gave him a big hug.

'What was that for?' he smiled at me, speaking quietly because I put my finger over my mouth to show that Dad was asleep.

'Dunno,' I whispered and we walked up to the loft, my hand comfortably inside his. That night as it got dark, Dad woke up and our parents argued. Or rather he spoke in a heated, confused voice and she tried to get him back into bed.

'Sorry,' we heard him say several times, loud and clear, 'I'm so sorry,' but the rest was mumbled and hushed. As their conversation became more irate, Rocco and I turned up the music on the radio and danced to it as if we were swimming under water, unable to hear or understand what was happening above the waves of lyrics and drums. We wore our mosquito masks and bounced on the beds, having a competition to see who could twist up and down the most times without toppling sideways and we pretended that we didn't hear Mum shout for Dad to come back as he left out of the front door. We even pretended that we didn't hear Mum run after Dad in the street, fragile female tears heaving from her chest. We didn't talk about it and, when we got up in the morning, Mum was sitting in a messier kitchen, eating cornflakes slowly and watching the television in her dressing gown. We didn't ask her what had happened, but a few weeks later we came home from school and found them lying next to each other asleep in bed. Rocco and I stood in the doorway to watch their chests rise and fall, their faces damp from tears and their skins white as household bleach.

Every day when I went to school the week after Jackson broke up with me, the creep didn't speak to me. He wasn't civil in the least, and when I tried to talk to him on his own he got embarrassed and turned his shoulders in my direction. I spoke to his back for a few minutes about him being stupid and it not being what he thought, but got bored with the lack of reaction and gave up. I walked off huffily like a girl is meant to when her boyfriend won't listen to her, and all the girls flocked round to tell me I could do better anyway and he wasn't as good looking as everyone made out.

Then Thursday morning I walked into a classroom and felt the conversation dry up. I looked up and then I looked down at my clothes. My skirt wasn't hitched up in my knickers, my tights weren't laddered, and my top looked fine. I didn't have any make-up on, so that couldn't be smudged, and I could feel my straight hair heavy around my waist.

'What?' I said sharply and everyone half-resumed their conversations. I walked over to sit with some people, two girls and three boys. Two of the boys repressed their laughter and bundled themselves out of the room as I blushed. The other boy was a quiet, studious boy with glasses who couldn't meet my eye. The girls looked up at me apologetically, but warily, disgust in their faces.

'Have you heard what Jackson said?' one of them said, looking at me with her big mouse brown eyes. She was a tiny, heavily tanned girl with a sharp chin and pointy nose. Her perfectly manicured nails were painted baby pink, which matched her eyeshadow. She crossed her legs twice over nervously and put her hands under her thighs. Then she took her hands out from under her legs and tucked her short brown hair behind her ears.

'I just got into school,' I said darkly. There was a very long pause as everyone in the room strained to talk and listen to our conversation at the same time. I raised my eyebrows and opened my sweaty clenched palms expectantly. 'What did he say?' I asked.

'He said that you and your brother . . . um . . .' she looked over to the side and then at my hands and then back up at me as if she'd just tasted sour milk.

I looked round the room nervously at all these people watching me. I wanted to be anywhere but there. 'Did he give any reason?' I stuttered, devastated. 'Or did he just think of anything he could to spite me?' I wanted to hit someone so much that my arm was almost rising in a fist by itself. I breathed deeply, and concentrated on staying composed and reasonable. Nobody would believe him, I repeated to myself as adrenaline spun through me again and I felt violent as an alley cat.

The girl mirrored me in my deep breathing, her chest rising up and down rhythmically. She came right up to near my ear, almost resting her chin on my shoulder. 'He said that when you first,' she coughed.

'When you, um, slept with him, you said you were a virgin.' She paused.

'Yeah,' I said, 'I was.'

'Well, yeah, everyone knows you didn't have anyone before Jackson and he says that when you had sex with him there wasn't any blood.'

The girl leant back against the locker she was sitting in front of, perched on a desk steady as a bird. She uncrossed her legs and then re-crossed them again while simultaneously brushing all her hair back with her hand. 'Nobody would believe Jackson over you, but as you were a virgin before Jackson, there simply has to be blood. Rocco's ex is backing Jackson, she says Rocco admitted that he fancied you and that's why they broke up. It's fucked up.'

'There was blood,' I said statically, feeling sick. The classroom was full. Everyone looked nervous, but excited and curious, giving me sideways glances.

'He says there definitely wasn't.'

'So you are taking his word over mine,' I said, looking cuttingly at her. I fiddled with my shoe, slipping it on and off.

'He also said he saw you kissing Rocco and that's why you broke up,' she continued.

'Rocco and I were fighting,' I said weakly and then I laughed, leaning my head back against the locker with a tight smile, remembering our stupid fight over the cigarette.

'Whatever,' she said and I suddenly couldn't breathe, so I walked out of the classroom while people erupted into questioning the girl while I was still within earshot. The word 'disgusting' rang out and I almost gagged from the repetition of the word. I walked quickly, very aware of my shoes clicking on the wet concrete outside and my hair ticking like a clock back and forward across my spine and of everyone staring at me. I went straight to the nurse in her little brick room and said in a small voice that I felt sick and could I please go home. I did feel sick, because what they said wasn't true. I'd never slept with Rocco.

The nurse had a very kind face, with a little bush of twig-like grey hair on her head and warm green eyes set very deep in her wrinkled face. She fussed around me and offered to ring my parents, to which I shook my head. She took my temperature, which was above average, and then sent me on my way.

'Don't you come back till you're better, young lady,' she said chirpily and so I walked home quickly, with no intention of ever coming back. Something definitely decayed inside me as I walked out of school that day.

When I got home Rocco was sitting in the dark living room, where the bulbs had blown and it smelt of soil from one of Mum's dead pot plants. He had placed the four officer soldiers in the middle of the dwarf coffee table and was drinking coffee with a map of London open across his knee, his fingers running across the little vein roads on the paper. That entirely drained feeling collapsed on top of me and Rocco looked up as I walked into the room with tears running down my face. He got up, knocking the coffee on to the carpet.

'What's the matter?' he said, looking scared and holding my shoulders as they bounced up and down. 'I bought you a present, Izzie,' he said imploringly, 'please don't cry.' I sat down on the sofa and curled my legs up towards my knees like a child. The torrent of sound coming from my mouth seemed to rip my throat and I hurled Rocco's coffee cup against the mantelpiece, breaking it. Rocco looked surprised, his eyebrows raising up his face and I crammed my fist into the cushions, shouting abuse.

'I was just thinking you looked a little stressed,' he said sarcastically, brushing my hair off my wet salty face. His thumb rubbed hard against my cheek and I noted that everything smelt organic in this room, of soil and salt. His fingers were comforting against my hot skin and I tried to breathe, as I watched him go into the kitchen and then return with his hands behind his back.

'I got you a mouse from the shop,' he smiled, taking a little cage from behind him and placing it on top of the coffee table so I could see a tiny white mouse asleep in a rubble of sawdust at the corner of the cage.

I made myself smile, although my lips felt like muscles after exercise, achy and unwilling to stretch. He opened the cage with a hook at the top and scooped up the little albino bubble of fluff in his big hands to place in my salty, shaking lap. The mouse woke up and looked alarmed, but I engulfed him comfortingly in my hands.

'Does he have a name?' I asked.

'We'll think of one,' Rocco said. 'Do you like it?'

'Of course,' I smiled, more willingly this time, because the mouse was nibbling at my shirt while I stroked his fur.

I looked down at Rocco's walking boots tied in a double knot. They had stepped in the spilt coffee and were now making footprints on the varnished floor. They were very old walking boots, grey with time and dust. His black trousers were fraying at the edges and only his studded leather belt around his waist looked sturdy. I breathed heavily and stroked the mouse. My breathing was beginning to regulate, although I had that acidic sickness beginning inside me and there was still a balloon of desperate adrenaline pumping up and up in the base of my stomach that I wanted to burst. I sat and stared with wet eyes at Rocco's features, which were bright with energy. At that point all I wanted was some coffee and a piece of chocolate cake, neither of which we had in the house.

—ᴍ—

Mouse

'Where do you think Mum and Dad have gone?' I asked Rocco, sitting on our balcony and stroking the mouse while looking out over Camden. I still felt as if we were living in an origami house, on a paper balcony.

'Your guess is as good as mine,' he said, turning his head away from me.

'I think fairies,' I said solemnly, pretending I hadn't noticed the reaction. 'I think fairies got bored in Cornwall and Ireland, so are slowly taking over the cities.'

'Perhaps we should cover the house in salt,' he said, 'I don't think fairies like salt.'

'They probably don't like cigarette ash or ancient Chinese food either,' I said. A pigeon ruffled its feathers, setting each one straight along its dirty back and watching Rocco take my hand in his. Camden looked like a brain or some sort of heavy robot stomach. I looked back up at Rocco, up to his lovely olive skin.

'Honestly Rocco, do you know why they left?'

Rocco looked sad, glancing at the floor and then the top right of the sky. I tried to read thought processes in his eyes and from the tilt of his lips, but he looked straight at me blankly and I shivered as he touched my neck, letting the very tips of his fingers run down my shoulder blade. I wonder if he knew, if he guessed, if he didn't want me to find out, if his suspicion was drifting irresolutely in his head like a body, but he wasn't thinking sharply enough to pin point the thought. He was letting the problem drift, his head half curious, half childishly scared. Or if he had persuaded himself he knew nothing more than me.

He touched my neck again just under my ear, so lightly that I could hardly feel it, and I turned away, nudging his fingers off my shoulder. The pigeon was standing right on the edge of the roof, looking down on us with its green eyes. There was still dried blood on the metal floor of the balcony, from where Rocco broke the glass, little splattered worlds like pigeon droppings.

'Do you think it's something to do with the shop?' I continued.

'What?' he said.

'I don't know, problems.' I leant forward, excitedly. 'Or maybe it's something to do with the guns.'

'I don't think so, it's probably nothing,' he said, and while I watched the pigeon totter around the rooftop preening itself like it was king of the world, Rocco watched a big man walk up the road towards our house.

'Do you remember when we found pills with long names on the kitchen table?' I asked.

'Not really,' he said uncomfortably. 'Most medicines have long names.'

The city was ashy and the cogs of it creaked, making me want to somehow erase it as if all we could see was an over-emotional oil-painted cityscape. I know that I'll go back to London one day if I can because it is the backdrop of my memories. Rocco blames things on cities, as if they were broken machines. He says the word London with the type of venom normally reserved for the word 'murder' or 'bomb'. Perhaps just as irrationally, I blame things on knowledge. I remember when Dad gave Rocco and I the sex talk. It was when I was seven and Rocco was nine. The whole scene is very vivid in my memory because I was expecting a considerably more shocking explanation for the violent panting noises we heard Mum and Dad making downstairs most nights. I really wouldn't have been particularly surprised to find that Mum and Dad tried to kill each other every night and the exertion of attempted murder somehow ignited a child in Mum's tummy once in a while. The real answer seemed tame, although Dad made a huge fiasco out of explaining it to us.

He *burst* into the loft one night, his cheeks blushing and his brow covered in a film of blue tinted sweat. He wasn't wearing his tweed jacket and his white shirt had ugly wet patches under his arms. I was sitting in the corner of the room playing quietly with my dolls and in Dad's hurry to get the conversation over with, he didn't notice that I was in the room. He hovered over Rocco's bed, heavy as a fat mosquito and I watched the male ritual with interest. Dad's arms stood static around his tummy as he described how to make babies in terms of bolts and screws, like bodies were some complicated bits of machinery that could link together if you followed the instructions carefully.

Afterwards he glanced around the room and his butterfly jumpy eyes rested on me and made his whole body jolt.

'Jesus Christ,' he said. 'Why didn't you tell me she was listening?' he looked accusingly at Rocco and me as we shrugged and smiled at each other. 'You shouldn't have listened,' Dad continued. 'It's not time for you to know all that yet. Your mother is going to kill me.'

Rocco reverted his eyes to the allure of the steady words on the page of his book, uninterested in the explanation.

'I didn't see you,' Dad almost whined, still standing nervously above us as he wiped the sweat off his long brow. 'You two are tricky children,' he said and made his way out of the loft, back to the safety of Mum's big warm body and wide painted lips.

Knowledge plays a large part in poisoning out innocence. In photos of me when I was younger, people say that I either looked lost or stoned. I have this vacant, blameless look. I almost always seem to be staring into space, as if I'm watching something really interesting in the far distance. You can almost see the purity leave my eyes if you put the few pictures Mum and Dad took of me in chronological order. You can see the knowledge build up in my eyes like silt. The more you know, the more you understand that the world isn't all that nice a place.

There is this one picture of me sitting in a wooden chair in Mum and Dad's bedroom when I was fourteen or so. Mum is brushing my very long glossy hair, holding all the shiny strands together in a fist behind my head and my face is covered in make-up. My cheeks are blushing, my lips turned on, my eyes outlined in thin charcoal and my freckles covered up by foundation that is slightly darker than my real skin tone so you can see the line like the edge of a mask. I have my hands placed primly in the ruffles of my floral skirt and I look unhappy, but expectant. I was going to my first disco that night and Mum had offered to get me dressed for it, a gesture I regretted accepting the moment she touched me. The foundation itched, the mascara was heavy and the powder made my eyes water. Just before I left, Dad got ill and Mum had to look after him, leaving nobody to give me a lift. Rocco was disgusted by my face and made me take off every bit of paint in front of the gilded mirror on the wall of the sitting room. I could see him in the mirror standing solidly behind me as I scrubbed my face, a look of severe but tender affection on his face. The make-up smudged and then I cried, making snail-trail streaks through the thick paint, and my brother kissed me on the forehead.

From the balcony we heard the big man Rocco had seen banging at the door. Neither Rocco nor I moved. The knocking continued and we stood very still, watching the limping pigeon.

'I'll go,' Rocco said.

'Don't open the door,' I said, but Rocco smiled and climbed back through the window to our room.

'Jesus Christ,' Rocco said, as he walked through the hallway towards the door. 'Ever heard of a doorbell?' he said, a little louder so that the man could hear. The door was shaking on the inside from being hit so hard.

'Wait, Rocco, please don't open the door,' I said nervously, standing on the bottom of the staircase, moving from foot to foot. The man's voice sounded parched like you'd expect a donkey to sound if it could speak English, quite unhealthy. Rocco put the chain on the door and opened it carefully.

'Hello?' Rocco said.

The man looked at my brother.

'The antique store is closed for the moment,' Rocco said before the man at the door began his sentence. 'If that is what you're waiting for.'

'So I understand, mate,' the man said, watching Rocco. 'But I'm not after antiques, mate, your father owes us money.'

There was a pause and then Rocco quickly closed the door.

The man pushed at the door. 'We're only going to cause you a hell of a lot of trouble if you don't pay,' he shouted and the pounding continued heavily on the door.

'We don't have any money, nothing,' Rocco said through the door. 'Go find our parents and tell them to pay our heating bill while they're at it.' We walked back up to the loft, and sat there without talking until the knocking subsided. I didn't say anything, money was becoming a problem that we didn't talk about. Rocco had a red face like poppies growing on each cheek. I lay down on my bed.

—ᴍᴍ—

BALLET

One night, as it began to get dark, Rocco and I ate a dinner of bread and cheese on the roof of our neighbour's house, within the territory of the limping pigeon who scowled at us under the shadows. We could tell that our neighbours were having a dinner party in the kitchen because of the noise through the walls and because there wasn't a light on in their bedroom like there usually was.

It was quite easy to climb across because of the balconies. Rocco did it elegantly, putting one leg on our balcony and one leg on theirs and then grabbing hold of their drain pipe and dragging his body slowly across. As he lowered himself on to their metal balcony, the pigeon took fright and wheeled up into the sky where it hovered angrily, blending into the oatmeal winter sky like a bit of fallen cloud. I passed

Rocco across the shopping bag of cheap champagne and food, which he placed on the floor at his feet.

'Are they in there?' I whispered to Rocco and he shook his head. 'What if they catch us?' I said.

'Nobody is going to catch me, lady, and make me a man. I always want to be a little boy and to have fun,' Rocco quoted.

'That's because as an adult you're a failure,' I said. 'But as a child you're spectacular.'

'I'll take that as a compliment,' he said as he helped me over the gulf between the houses, and then we climbed awkwardly up on to the tilted roof, grabbing at the drains, Rocco looking much more graceful and self-contained than I did.

Rocco and I both used to do ballet and Mum would drive us there dutifully every Saturday morning. It was a sparse, empty little room in the youth centre, with dirty floorboards and tarnished mirrors on every side. Rocco was the only boy in ballet class and at first he hated it, but he was very good with his body, much more elegant than me really. He eventually got thrown out because one day after class he got into a fight with one of the boys at the centre and broke his jaw. Rocco was only nine, but already had a violent streak.

After class we would usually go down to the canteen and have orange and biscuits with the rest of the group. Although Rocco liked the class, he didn't get on with any of the other people. The youth centre where the classes were held didn't just do ballet and most of the boys who attended played football or rugby, so at tea a group of boys would sometimes try and torment Rocco. They called him gay-boy or poet, and usually Rocco would just give them uninterested looks, but one time a whole group of them started shouting from the other side of the canteen, and one of them came forward, sticking his middle finger up at my brother. Rocco snapped.

Temper is one of those things you have to watch for, a kind of head chaos that you can't let show. Like hysterical giggles, crying and orgasms, losing your temper is an emotion nobody controls. It's what children do before they've learnt to structure their feelings. I imagine being in a war would be chaotic and subliminal. There would be no time to think, so you'd survive on temper and adrenaline. When I used to fight with Rocco on the floor of the loft, I'd get this rush of energy. Knobbly knees and nails and spit and knuckles all rubbing against each other giving adrenaline like an injection. The pain of his knee in the small of my back and the feeling of my nails scraping his skin was chaotic and full of red temper.

Rocco was always saying dramatic things. For example, at one point he claimed we were 'enslaved' by the guilt in human nature created by 'mankind's fall out of Eden'. Therefore all problems came from within people's own character and there were no outside forces like fate. I didn't really have a view on the matter, but if this was the case, then was mind chaos within or without the boundaries of character? Some people lose their temper more often than others, but we all have the childish capacity to be irrational and over intense. And we all get hysterical giggles and hysterical tears and although you can control it, sometimes the control has to snap.

Rocco looked terribly calm, but I knew that this structured tranquillity was Rocco's form of temper and I told him to stop, knocking over my drink as I did so. The boy was smaller than Rocco, with egg-yolk hair, and he was wearing a football shirt that was too big for him, while Rocco was in the baggy trousers and T-shirt that he insisted on dancing in. The football boy swung the first punch at Rocco, who proceeded to hit the boy under his jaw sending him reeling on to the floor.

'Rocco!' I shouted, annoyed, and as everyone crowded around the boy, Rocco came and picked up the tumbler of squash that I had dropped, replacing it in front of me on the table. I stood up and put my hands resolutely on my hips, feeling tearful.

'What did you do that for?' I said. 'Now we won't be allowed to come back.'

'He started it,' Rocco complained and I rolled my eyes precociously.

'We better go now,' I said, and we slipped out of the cafeteria and into the car park where all the parents were waiting for their children. We located our mother's little red mini and climbed into the back seat.

'I'm bored of ballet now,' I said to Mum as she passed us both tangerines to eat. 'Do you mind if we don't go next week?'

'Do you want to do something else?' Mum asked, as she tried to manoeuvre the car out of the parking space.

'No thanks,' Rocco said.

That was the end of our ballet careers, but neither of us really minded and we took up football at school after lessons instead.

Up on the roof, Rocco and I drank cheap champagne and talked about Mum and Dad.

'Do you remember Malta?' I said.

'I remember swimming in the sea,' he said. 'And I remember Dad breaking his leg.'

'Do you remember when Dad bought us the red masks at Christmas?'

'I remember we wore them all day and Mum got angry,' he said. 'We wouldn't eat the turkey because it was burnt and we knocked over the Christmas tree playing tag.'

'Do you remember the first time we heard them have sex?'

'No,' he said.

Camden Town was dark and we could hear the people underneath us clattering cutlery and talking between a fine wash of classical music that dripped out of the windows into the street in front of us. We didn't particularly like our neighbours, they had our telephone number for emergencies and were always phoning Mum and Dad to complain about the noise Rocco and I made with our radio.

The pigeon, still flapping in the sky, began to get tired and lowered himself on to the very top of the chimney where he sat and stared at us like a crow about to turn into a witch.

'If I could take away all your first times and put them in bottles I would,' Rocco said. 'Then I'd trap all mine as well and we'd both be little kids again, making mud pies in the garden.'

'I wouldn't,' I said. 'I'd trap the memory of them in glass jars, so I could experience them whenever I wanted, but I wouldn't wish that they hadn't happened.' I watched a double-decker bus rumble by, full of loud London people.

'So you do enjoy first times,' Rocco said almost accusingly. 'You really are stupid enough actually to want to grow up.' I wanted to run my fingers over the wrinkles of his frown and make them relax.

'I'd like to have all the adrenaline of childhood first times and never have to have to write a tax return,' I said.

'I expect that it's quite easy to remain a kid. If we're always together then we'll keep childhood habits and never grow up,' he said, taking a tentative sip of the slightly acidic, overly carbonated champagne.

'I'm going to be seventeen soon,' I said.

'You're stuck in a wasteland,' he said. 'Neither a child nor a woman.'

I frowned down at the tiles of the neighbours' roof. 'You're going to be nineteen. How about we ignore the rest of our birthdays? Nineteen is far too old for any child to be.'

We continued to talk about this for a while, about first temper, first blood, first kisses, and about our memories of Mum and Dad while we watched the city jumble below us and, when we heard people leave our neighbours' house, Rocco and I slipped back into the loft, where we went to sleep.

—ɯ—

STUFF

It only took one month for all this to rise, as if from the floorboards of our house. I suppose that the ground had been laid, the door unhinged with the slow build-up of the last three years. The last month that I'm writing about was perhaps just the outpouring of trapped temper. I spent quite a bit of time at the pet shop with Rocco over the next couple of weeks because I didn't want to be home alone, but I didn't want to be at school. I went in to register in the morning, usually planning to stick it out all day, but I tended to end up at the pet shop talking to Rocco around lunchtime and then not go back. I hated school even more than I disliked the smell of crickets and scales, so I sat in the back of the shop and read while Rocco worked. He shopped a bit, earned a bit of money, made sure we were just about OK.

'I saw Jackson today,' Rocco said one Friday when I turned up at about three o'clock, having stayed in school later than I would have liked so that I could have a flute lesson.

'Yeah? Did you talk to him?' I asked, looking up from my book. I was sitting next to tanks of baby spiders that the shop had bred. Tomorrow they were going to be separated from the mother in case she ate them and, although the bundle of little legs made me nervous, I'd never been squeamish about spiders. Rocco glanced at the babies and then back at me, sitting cross-legged on the dusty carpet.

'I said hello, we talked for a bit.'

'About me?'

'A bit,' he said. 'He was buying sandwiches with some friends.'

'Which friends?'

'I don't remember. You alright sitting there?'

'Wonderful,' I said, with a hint of sarcasm. I had to sit next to the spiders because it was the only place that was light; the rest of the shop was dark to suit the lizards and snakes. It was an artificial, cold sort of light that gave me a headache if I sat under it too long and which hit one of the tanks on the opposite side at such an angle that there was a shaft of white on the wall like a tear into another dimension.

'Do you speak to him at school?' Rocco asked me, and I shook my head with a shrug. When he left to look after a little-boy customer, I bit my nail while I read my book. At sixteen, I felt ten again and I had this childish irrational emotion in the base of my tummy. The same irrationality that used to turn shadows into ghosts, darkness into deadly gas and the rustling of the wind into stalkers. The spiders rustled next to me until six o'clock, when I helped Rocco close up the shop so we could go home.

Our house seemed desperate to fall apart; I'd never realised how much upkeep went into simply keeping a house running. There were nails sticking up from floorboards, broken pots, plates full of ash, sinks full of food and pans, cans on the floor, no food in the fridge, stray soldiers dead on their sides. The windows were dusty and frosted, the garden dead, the house cold as stone, and we had to drag the portable heater down from the loft and plug it into every room we spent time in. I felt like we were stuck on an unstable island in some huge throbbing lake, and every so often somebody would come round, knocking on the door and making the island sway. I couldn't understand why Mum didn't call.

When we got home, the elderly neighbour that I'd banished from the house previously was sitting at our kitchen table again and as I saw her I screamed, which made her almost fall off the chair. I'd become jumpy recently. The old lady had obviously just come, and she was half-heartedly trying to organise our kitchen table while still wearing her hat, gloves, coat and scarf because of the pinching cold.

'This is disgusting,' she said to us, almost venomously, as we walked in, and I felt a desperate desire to have her out of the house. Another presence in the house felt wrong, as if it changed the chemical balance of the air. In the kitchen the papers and school letters and catalogues and ripped envelopes were stuck together by spilt coffee, and although we did try to put things in the dishwasher after we used them, the sink was still full of cereal bowls caked in rock solid cornflakes and dirty water with stray french fries floating in it. We'd used up all the Fairy Liquid and it was too disgusting to begin trying to clean up now, so if we wanted to wash our hands we used the sink in the loo. The fridge was full of cheap Chinese food purchased from a take-away joint in Camden. At one point I was sure that the fridge was broken because all this clear liquid was dripping out of it, but Rocco smelt it and concluded that it was just a leaking bottle of 7-up hidden behind the Chinatown fridgescape. We'd stopped ordering food now and mostly ate sandwiches.

Outside in the garden, Mum's pots of herbs had frozen in their positions, their leaves like sharp icicles. It was strange, but we kept finding huge dead moths fallen frozen from the ceilings and I began to collect them in a shoebox. They literally froze out of the sky and fell heavy as bullets to the floor. It's amazing how many there were, and how big they got. My favourite so far was one the size of my thumb, which looked like a tiny bird. It was grey on the outside with a pattern of zigzags. Its body was like a furry frog with four amazing, long stick legs and then oversized brown wings hiding it all. The wings were fiery orange inside and a fine moth powder fell off when you touched them.

We had closed most of the curtains in the house to keep any heat inside, but it meant that moths got trapped between the icy glass and the curtain material. To add to the anarchy, a pipe had burst somewhere. I had taken to having long boiling baths in Mum and Dad's bathroom to calm myself down. Mum was big on bath salts, lavender and candles so their bathroom was like some oriental brothel, but very relaxing. You could curl up and lose yourself in steam, forgetting there really was a world outside. On Saturday I got out of the bath with all its bubbles and scent and wiped the mirror of its milky steam while grabbing a towel to dry my hair, which hung on to the damp heat while my body quickly cooled off. I pulled the plug of the bath and after a minute or so I heard a shout from downstairs. I put a towel around me and opened the door.

'What?' I shouted.

'There's water coming from the ceiling,' Rocco said.

'Where?' I replied, running down the stairs to see a

grey lightning split cracking the ceiling of the hallway and puddles of bubbly water all over the floor, discolouring the wooden boards. I laughed nervously and looked at Rocco. The ceiling looked as though it was about to discard plaster as well as water and we weren't sure what to do. We hovered under the vulnerable mosaic ceiling.

'Never mind,' Rocco said.

'Shit, Rocco,' I said, biting my nails. 'We're destroying the house, Mum and Dad are going to be angry.'

Rocco gave me this sarcastic, blunt look. 'I doubt a water pipe will be the most important thing on their minds.'

I looked up at my brother sharply. 'What do you mean?'

'Don't worry, that's all,' he concluded, turning around to signify that the conversation was over.

I had the feeling that the house should echo, although it didn't. Rocco had been reading me a book on Greek myths. Echo was a nymph who helped Zeus cheat on Hera and when Hera found out she punished Echo by making it impossible for her to say anything except the last words spoken to her. Later, beautiful Echo fell in love with the self-obsessed Narcissus and her unrequited love caused Echo's body to slowly disintegrate; it turned into shade and her bones into rock until only her voice remained. Echo should have taken up residence at our house, but instead a little

London nymph absorbed all our words, squashed them and kept them in Dad's ink pots in the sitting room. Everything we said felt pressurised to dust and inconsequential. I sometimes wonder if I am just an echo of Rocco, distorted a little by different genes, but fundamentally a repetition. One of the only interesting things I ever learnt in Physics at school was that bats, whales and dolphins use echoes to see the shape of sound. They give off vibrations and then judge their surroundings based on how much echo comes back to them. I would like to have some other sense, either an ability to feel echoes like a bat, or smell emotion like a beetle or read people's thoughts like a witch. I felt very trapped by our house. The walls seemed the wrong shape for the furniture, the ceilings too low for the walls, and Mum and Dad's jumbled possessions too numerous for Rocco and I to be in charge of.

'Sorry,' I stuttered to the old lady. 'I, um, said that I'd phone if I needed anything. We'd rather you didn't turn up unannounced,' I said. 'As nice as it is to see you.'

'Who is this woman?' Rocco said, turning to me and arching his eyebrows. I could see that he shared my need to be alone and isolated. Our neighbour's presence in the house made me nervous, despite what were obviously kindly intentions.

'I am Mrs Arnold,' she said.

'She's the neighbour Mum said would come and check on us once in a while,' I said.

'This must be Rocco,' Mrs Arnold said, pulling off one of her gloves in order to shake his hand. 'This place is a tip,' she said, looking around and straightening the stiff collar of her blouse. 'I do hope you two are OK.' The neatness of her blouse and heavy floral skirt looked odd in the centre of our clutter. Even her hair, which was turning grey at the roots, was doing so neatly.

'We are,' Rocco assured her. 'And as Isabel says, would you mind not turning up unannounced. It's slightly alarming to find someone sitting in our house.'

'Oh, dear, dear,' she said. 'Imagine finding me alarming? Aren't you jumpy. I'll telephone next time. I just wanted to check, you know, I promised to check.'

'Have you spoken to our Mother?' I asked.

'No dear, she didn't give me a number.'

'We'll phone if we need anything. Thanks for coming, but I'm afraid we have to get on with our . . .' he paused. 'Our homework.'

'Good. Do clear up,' she said as she left. 'This place is the messiest place I've ever seen. And cold. Goodbye,' she waved, slamming the door behind her and making Rocco and me laugh for the first time in a week.

The house was starting to make me feel displaced and emotional; it was too big and beginning to fall apart.

When Mum and Dad had sex loudly or argued, Rocco and I would sit in the loft with white spirit and matches, burning things. We knew that if they were involved in either of these mysterious activities they wouldn't be pedantic about the smell of burning in the air. Like all children, we were intrinsically interested in what burned and what didn't. We knew wood and paper burnt beautifully, exhaling this heavy clean smoke that filled up the room and stuck to the walls. We'd use a heavy blanket to put out the fire if it became too extreme, but we left it to the last available moment to get the most of the quick-paced, waxy energy adrenaline that pumped innocently through our veins, sharp as electricity. What was so lovely was the way it split in forks and you couldn't tell how it would ignite or in what direction it would singe.

We found that white spirit, easily stolen from a cupboard downstairs, would make any piece of material burst like a bomb. We burnt one of Mum's ugly silk scarves and it looked like an extension of the flames, wheezing an acidic smoke into the loft. Frail bits of old newspaper made a perfect flame, but however much white spirit you dripped on to the cold silver of a butter knife, metal wouldn't burn. A plastic bottle also wouldn't combust, but it did an amazing shrinking trick of folding inside itself and turning powdery black. Only once did we come close to damaging anything serious, and that was Mum and Dad's fault.

Downstairs they were eating each other's faces and pushing their white bodies against each other as if they were seasoning meat. Upstairs, Rocco and I were experimenting with whether fruit burnt, observing that it did so unsuccessfully. We had found a blanket somewhere by chance that was fire resistant and we had this on the floor under a small fire of school papers, on top of which we placed an apple and some plastic. The plastic bubbled like moon craters, or mud crawling with larvae and the apple shrivelled and turned black as the plastic melded on top. It gave off a terrible smell, which must have reached downstairs because, just at the climax of the flames folding over the apple, Mum and Dad burst into the loft in their dressing gowns.

Dad, his cheeks swollen, darted his skinny arm to the blanket and in a swift stupid moment ripped the blanket up from under the fire because he thought it was going to catch alight. He can't have thought the action through, however, and in the shifting smoky light Rocco and I sat aghast as our careful fire flew on to the corner of my duvet and began to burn.

'Stupid fucking children,' Dad said, as Mum stood helplessly in the doorframe as the duvet shrivelled and Dad kicked the bed angrily, just missing my hunched body on the floor. I put my face between my legs and tried to concentrate on not crying as Dad beat at the fire with my pillow. The fire got more irate, blooming over my bed. Then Rocco calmly took the fireproof blanket and smothered the blood-coloured flames so they disappeared under his firm hand. Even through the veil of smoke, Dad's face was bright and he kicked the bed over and over again before walking out of the smoke-filled room, followed tearfully by Mum. Rocco and I opened the window to let the smoke out and climbed out on to the balcony, bitter at the parental intrusion into our loft. We hated it when they came into the loft because they always caused some imbalance within the walls.

Now that Rocco and I were entirely alone in the house, we had begun to burn things again. When we used to be left alone for whole days we felt so small compared to the big house that our thoughts got larger than our bodies. Some writer said, 'Original sin is the property of the young,' but older people, solid bankers, lawyers, builders, accountants, sin too. But their sins aren't terribly original anymore. Whatever sins Mum and Dad may have committed, they certainly weren't unique. When you're young, each first sin has the originality of fire or snowflakes. Sin when you get older must become duller because you've read too many newspaper articles and under-stand the mechanics of death. When you're young you're innocent, but innocence doesn't guard you against your own sins. Aged seven, I hadn't yet really been polluted by media porn or violence, but I was fascinated by the fact that if somebody punched my leg it would ache and a poppy bruise would develop out of nowhere, and if I got a cut there was a sharper pain and wonderful bright blood. We would play games about tears and flames before we understood where tears and flames came from. We used to pretend that we were burglars, like Mr Curiosity from *Cats*. Little children who climbed through people's windows while they were sleeping, me in a dress, Rocco in jeans. We'd take pretty things we found, not money, and collect them all just like Dad collected his antiques. We pretended nobody suspected us because we were only children.

That night I went to the supermarket and bought eggs, ham and cheese to make an omelette. We tried to be civilised because I felt as if everything was falling over and tumbling down. I found a cookbook while Rocco set the table in the dining room with Mum's best china. He put out a cotton tablecloth with little yellow daisies in the corners and opened a new oatmeal coloured candle for the centre of the table. I tried to follow the directions for the omelette exactly, beating the eggs, chopping up the ham, adding the cheese to the saucepan at exactly the right moment, but I forgot to turn it round, so one side turned out charred.

Rocco laughed and I tried not to cry when he told

me it was fine, picking off the layer of black with a knife. I smiled at him, but felt sad at the silence in the house and useless because I hadn't made him anything nice. The problem was not that Mum and Dad were away, we didn't mind that; it was this heavy feeling that they weren't going to come back. The heaviness, darkness, and knowing that things aren't right.

The omelette tasted of soft yellow mud in my mouth, too buttery. I remembered one evening when we were younger and Rocco and I were both in naughty, fidgety moods because we hadn't been allowed to wear our mosquito masks at the dinner table. Mum was trying to tell a funny story about what happened at the supermarket and Rocco was staring at the counter behind my neck. Only Dad laughed at the punch line of her anecdote, then there was an uneasy pause as everybody turned to look at what Rocco was transfixed by. I edged around in my chair and saw two blue tinted spiders staring at each other. The smaller one slinked forwards, legs smooth as air over the white tiles, while the heavier one batted the air with its furry paws, lifting its legs rhythmically and caressing itself as it swayed.

'They want to have sex,' Rocco said, and I shot him a sharp momentary grin that quickly turned back to sombre concentration.

'Rocco!' Mum said, always pretending to be shocked by Rocco. 'Kill the horrible things,' Mum ordered

Dad, who rose from his chair obediently. Dad was wearing breeches, his face thin although not as thin as it got later, his hair grey.

The spiders moved towards each other, forward and then backwards as if losing nerve, each lunge of each limb somehow violent with their hairs on end. Dad faffed around to find a magazine as the spiders quite suddenly clung together with limbs everywhere, arching their legs painfully into a tangled web that rocked back and forward on the slippery tiles. Their fangs and blue tinted skin shook, vibrating, both straining their elegant little bodies as a shadow eclipsed them and then landed over their knotted bodies. Nobody dared pick up the paper again, but to Rocco and my distress, no mangled bodies clawed themselves to safety. There was a long pause.

Rocco and I turned our necks to look at Mum and Dad with our wide eyes even wider than usual, angry and surprised at this cruelty.

'You've sent them to hell just because they had sex,' Rocco said, young enough still to be caught up in the Sunday school moral that sex was a sin.

'There's no such thing as spider hell,' Mum said, staring nervously back at Rocco's angry face. She was wearing a blue checked dress with her hair pinned up above her ears.

'If there's a human hell, there must be a spider hell,' Rocco said.

'Then all spiders go to hell,' Mum said weakly.

'Bullshit,' Rocco said, not breaking her gaze. Dad was hovering above me, fondling the offending magazine and looking like a guilty hit-man.

'Go to your room,' Mum said, folding her napkin.

Rocco pushed his chair carefully from the table, placed his knife and fork together and walked out of the door. I waited a second and then did the same because Mum and Dad looked shaken.

'Get back here,' Mum said as I left, but I ignored her. I never really came to blows with Mum and Dad, but at an early age always tended to side with my brother. I would have been alarmed by Rocco, if I were Mum and Dad, but like me, Rocco objected to how our parents wanted their children to behave. They wanted blonde ringletted children who could be silenced by lollipops and make attractive family photos. However, they didn't set the angel example terribly convincingly.

After picking at the omelette, Rocco and I went up to bed, slightly hungry although neither of us would admit it, and as he got changed for bed I noticed that his knuckles were red, as if he had hit something.

15

—ᗡᗡ—

JACKSON

The first time Jackson kissed me I was convinced that I was going to break. I was practising a flute piece in one of the little music rooms that I liked to lock myself inside, playing the same bit of the same tune over and over until the sound of it filled up my entire head, letting out little bits of whistling atmosphere. At first I didn't hear Jackson knock, thinking that the sound was just a floorboard creak or something falling in the hallway, but then he was standing in the doorway grinning at me and the trap doors of my flute creaked and screamed a nervous high note. I took the flute from my lips and placed it neatly on my lap, looking up at Jackson with my eyebrows raised. I was wearing a black jumper with a V-neck, a pleated black skirt and tights that suddenly felt quite itchy against my legs. All his hair was sticking up awkwardly to the right, making his sharp face seem lopsided, and his floppy trousers were dragging over his big shoes.

'Hi,' I said, tingling and twisting the bits of the shiny metal stick away from each other and cleaning the insides with a felt straw, pretending there was something wrong with it. The flute was slippery on the outside and tarnished and tight at the joints, but the red felt slid easily up it and made the insides shine while he watched my thin hands flicker.

'Am I interrupting?' he asked politely.

'It doesn't matter, I was just practising.'

'You're good,' he said and I squinted slightly, wondering where this was going. 'I was listening outside,' he admitted.

'Thanks,' I said, putting bits of the flute back together and standing up to get the case from the other side of the room. Jackson went to the other side of the room and looked at me.

'Look, can I say something?' he said quickly.

'I guess,' I said, and turned to face him, my hands hanging statically at my sides. I felt badly proportioned and all the wrong shape within the perfect square of the little shoebox music room, which smelt of carpet and perfume. Jackson looked at me.

'I think that, well, I think it's good how you don't care what people think of you. I think we could be really good together.'

I smiled willingly at him, but looked confused so that he would make himself entirely clear.

'Would you go out with me sometime?' he continued.

'Um . . .' I faltered, feeling ecstatic and pretty and scared all at the same time.

He walked over to me and put his hand round my waist with his thumb cold on my front and the rest just reaching my spine over my jumper, resting there between the bones of it. Then he tilted his head to the side and moved it forward a fraction to kiss me, lips hitting lips like he was pressing in arsenic through the crack, which sped straight to my head and created puddles of air in my instantly unbalanced knees. His tongue crept into my mouth and I opened my lips a bit more, kissing him nervously back, and as we drew apart for a second he said he loved me and I smiled through the gauze of lips and adrenaline. That was the only time he ever said that he loved me, but it was a charming moment.

I'd kissed other boys before Jackson. I'd kissed Rocco, a boy at a camp I went to one summer and a boy at a party, but none were quite like this. If I were to be absurdly accurate about my emotions, I did love him, but it was a love I now know was hopelessly naive and badly formed. The first time you 'fall in love' it's very difficult to know whether you are actually in love, because you have nothing to compare it with. I don't think I've ever been truly in love with anyone but Rocco, not even now, months after Jackson left me standing barefoot in my pyjama shorts on the snowy road for no good reason.

Eventually I disliked him a lot more than I'd ever liked him. Jackson didn't have charm, that elusive and slightly sinister characteristic that makes you adore someone. He had a cold kind of teenage quality that made him popular, a cigarette hanging limply from his lips most of the time, a slight uncaring slouch and a dragging quality to his walk, which is almost the teenager's version of charm, but hardly magnetic. He had a sharp tongue and social intelligence, but he wasn't charming like Rocco could be when he wanted.

Still, I wish I could trap that one charming moment with Jackson in a viscous blue liquid, the colour of cool thoughts and the middle of a flame. I'd put a drop in my cereal every day and always be quite happy, or I could save up litres and litres of ecstatic moments and overdose myself with youth when I wanted to die.

⚊⚏⚊

16

PARENTS

Three weeks after Mum and Dad left we still hadn't heard from them so Rocco and I went down to their empty room, which smelt of floral scent, and I felt we were eavesdropping again. At first I didn't want to go down, but once Rocco went I followed him into their horrible scramble of private possessions.

Their bed was unmade so we could still see the creases in the bed from where Mum slept the night before she left, like she had mislaid her shadow in the rush to leave. Mum slept on the left, Dad on the right. There was a yellow-tinted light shade to the right of the bed and a mismatched antique painted one to the left. One of them had a crack down the side, as if it had fallen or been thrown, but it was glued back together. There were dresses on the bed, underwear on the grey-carpeted floor, and other remnants of the quick exit Mum had made. To the right of the bed was a medium-sized window with pollen-coloured curtains that matched one of the lampshades. There was a desk that Mum and Dad shared, which was usually neat, but today cluttered. I kept getting horrible split second flashbacks of Mum and Dad fighting. The images were gone in a second as if they hadn't come, but they left me dizzy.

Rocco and I stood in the middle of the room and breathed the flowery smell deeply, both wishing we were back in our own room where we understood the dramas detailed in the chaos. I picked up one of Mum's dresses and ran the smooth hemline between my fingers comfortingly, while Rocco leafed through some of the papers at the desk, both of us feeling like guilty children. There was still a broken plate on the floor, looking as if it had been thrown.

Rocco removed the drawers of the desk, which were loose and slid open easily. It was a well-made, dark mahogany desk with a stained beige leather top. Inside were pens, crayons, plasters peeking out of their plastic wrappers, broken cigarettes, a pair of dice, some loose change and Mum's old fat address book. Rocco carefully picked up the full, papery book and turned a few pages while trying not disarrange the yellowing papers, before passing it to me. This was the address book Mum had used since she was twenty-four, beginning in round letters dotted with hearts or smiley faces and gradually transforming into tighter, more scrawled notes and lines of figures. In the first half, the pages detailed dinner dates and telephone numbers, progressing into the addresses of plumbers and national insurance numbers. There were smiley faces doodled next to certain people's names and a lot of exclamation marks. 'Meeting Clare for coffee! Don't forget!' 'Book dentist appointment!' Near the end were sums, scrawled out, circled, underlined and the whole thing scratched black so the process could be begun over again underneath. I didn't bother to do the numbers, saving them for a more tranquil moment in the loft where I wouldn't be distracted by the sad lingering smell of perfume around us. Instead I closed the book and put it on the corner of the desk. I also removed a crumpled, tall pile of heavily fingered bills from the second drawer down, flattening them with my fingers and folding them on top of the address book before walking over to Mum and Dad's gaping wardrobe.

I looked at the unorganised row of skirts and suits hanging inside. There were quite a few of the loose, floral linen and silk dresses Mum always wore, the kind with a square neck and a low belt hanging over the hips. There were some still in their plastic cocoons from the drycleaner's and at the bottom were a jumble of Mum's and Dad's shoes. I took a hat off the shelf above the clothes and put it on my head. It was a floppy black one, made out of a material like felt that heated up my head and made my hair feel static. The edges wilted slightly down over my eyes, soft as a petal, and I pushed it back up so I could look up under it at Rocco. It had a white rim around the edge and an embroidered pink rose on the right hand side that was hanging limply from the couple of strands of thread Mum had obviously used to fix it at some point.

Rocco came and looked over my shoulder into the wardrobe while I sat down on the bed in Mum's hat. The sheets were all crumpled under me and I felt like I shouldn't be sitting there, ruining the dips in the sheets that Mum and Dad used to occupy. I ran the warm corners of the sheet through my fingers and watched Rocco fondle two of Dad's cufflinks, embossed in gold with the initials Z and M, which Dad had bought from a vintage clothing store. Rocco put them on to his shirt carefully through the yellowing button-hole.

'I like these,' Rocco said, and I nodded. I don't remember having been in their room without them being there for years. Obviously we sometimes went in, to tell them that the telephone was for them or that we were going out, but it was always an awkward kind of quiet hovering at the door. We said our bit and exited swiftly, because we disrupted the dynamics of their relationship as they did ours. Mum would be sitting with her legs crossed where I was sitting and

Dad would be leaning on the edge of the desk, inclining forwards towards Mum, looking intent. Then we would walk into their simmering air space and unbalance the mixture of endorphins and adrenaline in the air, so that the conversation would fragment.

Rocco rummaged through Dad's clothes, looking for anything of interest, and eventually dislodged a brown jacket from its hanger and put it on the bed next to me. Then he knelt down, moving a few shoes away from the floor and picked up a box decorated with yellow paint. I noticed that he remained, kneeling, his back to me, for an elongated moment, but when he came up with the box I thought no more of it, figuring that the situation was making me over-sensitive. That night, however, I re-remembered the moment and wondered tiredly what he had moved in the wardrobe, what he might not be saying.

Rocco sat next to me on the bed and nudged off the little wrinkled lid of the box, and took out a tacky plastic pink bracelet, which I slipped on to my wrist so that the pale beads pinched my skin. There was a black fountain pen, a broken pencil sharpener and a rock.

I giggled at the sight of Rocco wearing Dad's jacket and I picked up Mum's silk dressing gown from the floor, putting it on over my clothes and tying the white belt tightly around my waist. I coughed and began to place pins in my hair, like Mum was always doing.

'I hate London,' I said, because Mum was always saying that and I tried to put on Mum's nervous voice.

'Well, we can't move,' Rocco said, making his eyebrows dance and standing limply with his shoulders hunched, hands in his pockets. 'Madame Malcontent,' he added, because Dad often called our mother that.

'I wish the shop was doing better,' I complained, biting my lip.

'It pays the bills,' Rocco replied.

'Sometimes,' I said sadly, running the hem of Mum's dressing gown between my fingers. 'But it would be nice to have enough money to give a bit to the RSPCA once in a while.'

Rocco grinned at me, because I sounded quite a bit like Mum, still trying to pin my hair unsuccessfully.

'You never buy anything that we can sell, Jack, nobody wants what you like. The entire world isn't obsessed by war memorabilia,' I continued. 'People like pretty things, not violent things. We should start a greeting cards store. Everyone likes greetings cards.'

'I don't,' Rocco said, lighting up a cigarette in Dad's shaky, tortured manner as if he was scared of his own skin.

'And the kids!' I said, smiling. 'Those terrible kids!'

Rocco laughed. 'Always sneaking about!'

'Now Rocco doesn't go to school he's going to be working in a pet shop all his life,' I said. 'And Isabel is so surly, following her no-good brother around, never doing anything constructive.' I frowned, alarmed by my own accuracy, my own imitations.

'I love you,' Rocco said in a cartoon voice. 'Love you more than the world.'

'I love you too,' I said, putting my hands to my heart and Rocco tipped ash on the carpet.

'Don't tip ash on the carpet Jack,' I reprimanded, tugging at the belt of the dressing gown as it slipped away from the knot.

'Don't tell me what to do,' Rocco said, mock angrily.

'Somebody has to. Somebody has to tell you to step out of yourself and notice that you have two children that you won't touch and that the shop never sells a single fucking thing.' I flicked my hair theatrically and with a grin Rocco took the broken lamp from next to Mum's side of the bed and dropped it on the ground so that it made a splintering, jagged noise on the floor, splitting in a million pieces.

The whole room went very silent as we both looked at the broken china lamp. Rocco stubbed out his cigarette on the floor slightly sadly while I took off the dressing gown. In the quiet, I put the pillows of the bed in their right places and smoothed the duvet, rubbing out Mum and Dad's shadows before folding up the dressing gown and placing it neatly on the bed.

'Do you feel sick?' I asked Rocco.

'Sort of,' he said, and we walked out of the room. In the doorway I stood for a moment and grabbed the bracelet to tug it off my wrist, but it broke and the beads scattered into the crevices of the room, making a noise like hail on a window at night. I didn't look back to see where the beads fell, and we closed the door and ran up to the empty loft.

—m—

SCHOOL PROBLEMS

I didn't look down in the wardrobe, because I felt pathetically nervous. As children Rocco and I didn't look at anything we didn't want to see. We looked at blood, spiders, tongues, because they were disgusting in a stunning way, but anything dull or complicated we resolutely ignored. I was not an adult at sixteen, some people might be, but the fact that I didn't march straight down to the wardrobe shows that I was still trying to survive in a badly erected den made out of fresh linen, wax crayons and Lego pieces. I didn't want to grow up, not just then.

I hadn't been going to school much, but just enough to stop any inquiry. Everyday I stayed home, Rocco phoned me in sick, pretending to be Dad. When I did go to school I was almost entirely ignored. While Jackson put all his effort into rallying himself into the position of victim, I was silent. I left school whenever I felt like it; I got sent to the headmaster's office for not doing my work and I didn't try to argue my point. They kept phoning home and Rocco would tell them with a tone of authority that his daughter was doing fine and could they please leave her alone. Jackson put a picture of Rocco and me on the notice board, taken when we were both drunk and he happens to be glancing down my top. People covered it in rude graffiti and although I took it down and threw it away several times, Jackson always seemed to have a convenient copy.

I had one conversation alone with Jackson. He came up to me while I was eating lunch in the neon-lit food hall at school, idly dragging his feet as he always did. He asked if he could talk to me for a minute in private. It was in the middle of the room and everyone nearby looked around, so I nodded submissively and followed him into a classroom.

'Hi,' was his opening line as he closed the classroom door and perched on the edge of a wooden desk. He had a fading bruise on his left cheek, which his blonde hair could not hide. The classroom had three rows of wooden desks and a set of aluminium-framed windows at the back, which looked out over the back of the school and the triangular wire fence. On the same wall as the door were silver and grey lockers with people's names scratched in them. The whole room was washed through with light from the three rods of cheap lamps that didn't really cast shadows, but instead, like magic, just made the whole room two-dimensional.

'Hi,' was my answer. I flipped my hair over my shoulder nervously and stood straight as an arrow in front of Jackson, thinking about how much I hated him.

'You don't look good,' he said, fidgeting with the metal hinges on the table. That morning, looking at myself in the mirror, I'd noticed how my skin looked taut and thin, as if it had collected a fine layer of dust.

'Really?' I said. I glanced out of the window into the snowy concrete streets, then looked back at his shifty face and watched his hand in his pocket twist the long black lighter that he always used. 'Nor do you,' I said, pointing at the bruise on his cheek.

'You know who did that?' Jackson asked. 'Your fucking brother, last week, and it still hasn't gone down.'

'I didn't tell him to do that,' I said. 'I didn't know he had.'

'It was all playing with my head, Isabel,' he said. 'You two sitting there juggling with guns and watching pigeons fight, then you get up and get changed in front of us. It struck me that you probably got changed in front of him all the time. Then I walk in and you are about to kiss him.'

I smiled at Jackson, looking up at him through my eyelashes and hating him. 'You know we weren't about to kiss, you're being dramatic.'

'No, I'm not,' he snapped at me with force in his voice. 'It's disgusting. You two in the same room every night, nothing to do, both want a fuck, so you fuck.' Jackson took the lighter out of his pocket and began twisting it around in his fingers, pulling it through the sweaty skin between his thumb and forefinger.

'We didn't invite you to be a part of it,' I said, raising my eyebrows, and Jackson's flushed cheeks became paler. His fidgeting was beginning to annoy me.

He stood up and walked over to the door, absently putting the lighter down on the table. I leant on the cold grey lockers and unclenched my hands. My heart was beating fast and I remembered the feeling of him drawing up the inside of my thigh.

'You didn't have to tell the whole school,' I said. 'You could have stopped hanging out with us without spreading ugly rumours.' I stopped fiddling with my hair and looked at him pointedly. He lowered his eyes. 'Did you just get bored after I slept with you?' I asked.

'No,' he said. 'I don't know. There was something about sleeping with you that made me think you'd practised already.'

'What?'

'It just felt dirty.'

'Dirty?' I said.

'I started to notice how you touched him and how he watched you.'

'That's dumb, Jackson.'

'I just stopped wanting to be around you,' he said, turning slightly, digging the rubber of his shoe into the floor.

'You told the whole school,' I repeated.

'I could tell the police,' he said. 'That shit is illegal.'

'It's not true,' I said.

'It is,' he said, and I felt the sting of tears behind my eyes. His blonde hair was flopped over his eyes and his skin was getting progressively paler, his thin mouth arched into a bowstring frown. His blue eyes were almost white, the colour of transparent tinted plastic. I'd never noticed before, but the skin on the back of his arms was almost translucent white. I looked down at the veins sliding around under the thin skin of his wrist. Then I looked back up at Jackson through the film of glue-like moisture in my eyes.

'Look, Isabel,' he said, slower now, and I tried to stop myself from thinking about the night we slept together. Him standing in front of me like this, self-conscious, made me remember how I felt the night in the loft before I got the cream feeling inside me. The trouble with memories of irrational actions not backed up by thought, is that they aren't steady. It's like when you're a child your memories mutate and warp due to how you're feeling at the time, so something which was perfectly pleasant can muddle into something catastrophic simply because you're thirsty or you woke up too early that morning. I felt like that now, as if that whole scenario had been unsatisfying and embarrassing. I felt a sickness begin to blossom in me, but tried to quench it, remembering that I was judging it in retrospect. Rocco once told me about a philosopher called Emmanuel Kant who enthused that the only thing that we could create morality from was reason, and anything unreasonable was immoral. In a way this is true, so much of what is irrational could also be argued to be immoral, but then irrational things are often the most fun.

'Isabel,' Jackson began again slowly, looking first at his feet and then almost to my face, but a little to the right so it gave the impression that he was looking with a glazed expression over my shoulder. 'I am actually sorry that this worked out how it did, because I did really care about you. You were sweet, but you are his. When you're with Rocco everything just becomes, different. I didn't want to care about something, which was, well, not right.'

'I was always with Rocco, I always am with him. He's my brother.'

'I know,' he said. 'And I don't like you two when you're together. Rocco isn't right.'

'I love him. I don't care about you, Jackson,' I said.

There was a pause and I noticed how stuffy the

classroom was, smelling of little boys and new paint. The white light gave the classroom a gutted, empty feeling as if the whole place was clean and dry as powdered disinfectant. Jackson glanced straight at me and there was half a moment when we shared a look, almost like we used to, but then Jackson left the room with a theatrical flick of his hair.

'Jackson, wait,' I said and he turned around. 'Sorry he hit you,' I said.

'I'm not,' he replied, squinting at me. 'Gives me proof.'

In the hallway I heard people ask him questions about what I'd said and if I'd admitted it. Disgusting, disgusting, disgusting was the only word I could hear. I flicked the lighter Jackson left on the desk sadly and watched the pretty flames jump up to try and touch my face. I felt messy, disgusting.

I walked home quickly and I could feel someone following me. I knew it was a man because his foot-steps were heavy with the flat sound of men's rubber soled shoes and it certainly wasn't Jackson's footsteps. He walked just behind me for almost a minute, quite close to me on the thin street, but of course I couldn't turn around. I didn't think anything, but I felt nervous because I could almost feel his body heat in the sharp cold.

As I walked through one of the empty streets near

our house, the man behind me quite smoothly put his arm over my right shoulder and turned me around while simultaneously wrapping my left hand behind my back. He hurt me and I tried to scream, but only a muffled sound came out. I squirmed sideways and dropped my school bag. Adrenaline filled up my veins, but I couldn't move. The sockets of my arms hurt and I stamped on his foot, but he pushed me away like I was a doll. He pressed me up against the wall, putting his hands over my neck and pinning me so I couldn't move. My coat was slipping off my shoulders and I felt like some frozen Neolithic animal, cold and paralysed. I squirmed over and over with my hips, but seemed to stay in exactly the same place.

'I'm not going to hurt you,' the man said. 'Stop squirming. His breath smelt of garlic and toothpaste. I could see him very clearly, he was the big man who had knocked on our door previously. His skin was rough and dimpled like a naked sheep, his eyes tiny little slits in his forehead. 'Just tell me where your parents have gone,' the man said gruffly, letting go of me a bit so I could talk.

'I don't know,' I said. 'I really don't, if I knew I'd be with them. We're worried, we haven't heard anything since they left and we don't have any money.'

He let go of me abruptly and walked off. I stood stunned for a minute and then made my way home, slamming the door, which seemed to have been slammed rather a lot lately. After that I began to skip school more than ever, my motivation dramatically declining.

On Thursday the doorbell rang and Rocco wasn't in, but I didn't move to get it at first. I had taken the mouse from the cage and was drinking coffee while stroking it and watching television in the loft. There was a ten-minute pause and then the doorbell rang again. I took another sip of coffee and lit a cigarette, putting the mouse in my pocket. On the television a group of gothic dressed teenagers were talking about why they wanted to have babies, and their bleary eyed parents, sitting nervously next to their offspring, looked like pigeons who had given birth to hyenas. The mothers seemed alarmed by the whole situation and shocked that they had bred children who made such incoherent arguments. One small, blonde girl of about fifteen and her weedy boyfriend could hardly string a sentence together under the gasps and booing of the live audience, but nevertheless they put up quite a good fight. They were ready to start a family, the boy had a steady job on a construction site, the girl was feeling broody. Then there was another, slightly older, fatter girl, telling everyone how she got pregnant at fifteen and it ruined her life.

The doorbell rang again, and the person also knocked authoritatively on the door three times, so I wandered down the stairs to look through the peephole to see who it was. Far from being a debt collector looking for Dad, the man standing at the door was just my English teacher, an enthusiastic grey-haired man called Mr Brown who was standing a couple of steps away, looking searchingly up at the windows above to see if there really was nobody home. I thought about leaving it and hoping he'd go away, but Mr Brown had always been quite nice to me so I opened the door for him. He was wearing what he always wore, a dingy brown suit with a thin stripy shirt and a plain coloured tie. Today the tie was blue, and it was knotted too tight underneath his neck.

'Oh, hello,' he said, and I suddenly realised that I couldn't let him in the house because he'd see what a mess it was and how it smelt. I wondered if he would tell me to put the cigarette out. 'I thought perhaps you weren't home,' he said.

'Sorry,' I said, sucking on the filter of Rocco's Marlboro red. 'I couldn't hear the bell.'

'I was wondering if I could come in and talk to you and your parents about your absence from school. Nobody has been picking up your telephone.'

I wished I hadn't opened the door, as much as I liked Mr Brown, because I wasn't sure what I was going to do now. It seemed odd not to let him in, but above all I didn't want anybody in the house. It was our house now, and another presence might make the whole place crumble. It was only just about staying up with Rocco and me in it. He brought back horrible memories of school and Jackson.

'Sorry,' I repeated dumbly. 'Mum and Dad aren't here at the moment.'

'Can I come in, or do we have to have this conversation on the doorstep, Isabel?' he said and I looked back to the hallway, with its puddle of water and stench of weed and greasy rice. The weather outside was cold, however, and I didn't know what to do so I continued to hover where I was. There was a pause as nobody said anything. 'Where are your mother and father?'

'They've gone away,' I said, stubbing out the cigarette on the doorstep and taking the mouse out of my pocket, making Mr Brown's eyes squint.

'Where have they gone? Isabel, I think we need to get hold of them.'

'*We* can't even get hold of them,' I snapped, stroking my mouse, whose whiskers twitched. 'So if you get them, could you tell them to ring us?'

'Is something the matter?' Mr Brown said. The mouse's fur was soft, making me feel calmer. 'Would you like to see a counsellor, if you won't talk to me?'

'I'm fine, thanks,' I said.

'Are you ill?' he said, and I shook my head. 'Are your parents ill?' he continued and I shrugged my shoulders. I saw Rocco walking back from work. He looked inquisitively at me as he turned up behind the teacher.

'It's Mr Brown,' I said in answer to my brother's look. Mr Brown turned around and smiled at Rocco, who shook his hand.

'Nice to see you, Rocco,' Mr Brown said blankly. 'Can I come in and talk to you? Isabel hasn't been attending school and we're all a bit worried about her.'

'She was being bullied,' Rocco said. 'So she's left.' Rocco walked past me into the door and I stepped back into the hallway. 'I'm sorry if she's caused any trouble, but she won't go back. Thanks for coming over and all, it's really nice of you, but she can look after herself.'

'It's a very bad idea for her to give up school,' Mr Brown said.

'Yes, well, things don't always go to plan, do they Mr Brown?' Rocco said.

'Where are your parents?' Mr Brown asked again.

'They're on holiday. Look, Mr Brown, I'm eighteen and perfectly able to look after us both,' Rocco said.

'Your parents won't be impressed when they come home and find that their daughter has followed in her brother's footsteps,' Mr Brown said.

'No, perhaps not, but a lot of stuff has been happening and she just can't face school at the moment.'

'Can I just please come in and talk this over with you?' Mr Brown said.

'I don't think there is much else to say. Sorry you had to come over here for nothing.'

'If she's not back in a week she'll probably be expelled, Rocco,' Mr Brown said, and then he looked over Rocco's arm to say goodbye to me and I waved half-heartedly at him, so relieved now that he was going and so happy that I wasn't going back to that horrible school.

'Rocco?' I said, deciding not to tell him about the man on the street for fear of scaring him, 'You didn't hit Jackson, did you?' I asked sharply.

'Sorry Izzie,' he said, and I scowled at him angrily, stroking the mouse in my hands and staring at my brother for a moment before going to put the mouse back in her cage and have a shower.

For the next couple of days I was cold with Rocco, talking to the mouse, who nuzzled at me and never did anything wrong.

'Isabel, I'm sorry,' he said. 'He's a jerk, he made you sad and I couldn't bear it.' I was lying on Mum's bed in their bedroom, where I had come to get away from him. I still hadn't looked in the wardrobe, but was smoking a cigarette with the mouse crawling nervously over my stomach.

'It proved his point, not ours,' I said.

'I don't do things to prove points. He asked for it and I don't believe you really care, so don't be dramatic. He hasn't made the last few weeks easy, has he?' He stood in the doorway for what seemed like forever as I stroked the mouse and inhaled deeply. 'I'm sorry,' he repeated sadly. 'I'm sorry about all this. I hate to see you looking sad or nervous. I'm not looking after you properly, it's pathetic,' he said, running his fingers through his hair and I allowed him a slight smile.

'Think of the big houses in Camden like that big white one with a BMW in the driveway,' Rocco said eventually.

I nodded.

'Wouldn't it be easy to work out when they were out and slip in one night, just take a couple of hundred pounds from the father's stash and slip off again without moving anything? They might not even notice, we'd be invisible.'

I smiled and then laughed for a moment. Last night I had dreamt about Mum and Dad. Dad had been all dressed up in white and he couldn't see Mum even though she was standing right in front of him. Then Dad started to scream and I woke up sweating.

'Couldn't we borrow some money from the old lady?' I said carefully, fraying the corner of an old newspaper. Rocco looked at his knees. 'Besides, we've got your pay.'

'We need to start paying the bills,' he said, sitting down on the bed and unfolding a map on his knees and pointing with his wide steady finger to a road just near us down in Camden. 'It would be interesting to break in. What do you think?' Somehow the way he said it and the way he looked with his sturdy smiling mouth and thoughtful green eyes, it sounded like a reasonable idea.

I looked down and noted that my hand on Rocco's leg was shaking slightly from the exertion of thought. 'It is easy to escape daylight,' Rocco said, putting his hand on mine over the mouse, 'but night is inevitable, and dreams are the giant cage.'

'Who said that?' I asked Rocco.

'Truman Capote,' Rocco said.

I felt exasperated by the whole situation. More frozen moths had begun falling from the grooves in the ceiling and the shoebox was becoming cluttered. The oldest moths had lost their structured energetic beauty and the powder from their wings scattered the grey base of the box. I shifted them with a bit of card to make it so that none of them were on top of any of the others, but one of them fell apart, wings cracking at the base and the powder soft as cigarette ash. One of the lovely things about the soldiers was that they were as pretty as the moths, but wouldn't change or decay. I wondered if moths had blood in them like humans.

Our Grandfather, the one who died of cancer, used to swear by nettle tea. He used to say, 'Do you know why I'm still as sharp as I was when I was at school? Nettle tea.' One day, in the middle of the summer holidays when there was nothing to do but find obscure ways to amuse ourselves in the garden and try not to annoy Mum and Dad, Rocco and I picked all the nettles from the rims of the flowers. We wore big gloves, the kind with fat fingers and elastic wristbands to rip the nettles out of the earthy ground. Our little garden was full of nettles, sinister prickly stems of green nodding their heads from under the dripping purple flowers and eyelash daisies. We collected a big pile on the wall of the garden and then smashed them all up with a wooden spoon until we got a veiny green pulp that stained the bottom of the mug and soaked into the wood of the spoon.

Then Rocco boiled the kettle and we brought the mug of pulp into the kitchen to pour water on. Of course then we had a mug of green water with goo in it, so we cleverly sieved it with Mum's silver tea strainer until we had another mug of marshy green water. By this point the water was cold, but we sipped it anyway; it tasted like watery grass, not very life-enhancing at all. I wanted Grandpa to come back, he always knew what to do and there were so many basic things that I still didn't understand. For example I didn't really understand what a mortgage was, or how to cash a cheque in a bank, or change a tyre. Grandpa had always been worldly, while the rest of us really weren't.

*

Rocco came up behind me while I was brushing my teeth in the bathroom mirror and put his hands around my waist. He had been making little tours to the white house and telling me his plans when he got home. Telling me when these people went out, when there was nobody in the house. He used to steal things as a child, just to see if they would catch him, but they never did. Gum, magazines, cigarettes, ice cream for me, never anything big.

'We have everything we need,' he said on Friday night.

'Tonight?' I said, scared.

'The man seems to be away for the weekend and the woman goes out on Friday night.'

'You've been watching?'

'Yes,' he said.

'Kids?' I said, after I spat the toothpaste out. I washed the brush and put it back in the little cup. I then bent down to fit my mouth under the tap and take a sip of water. I spat that out too and looked round to Rocco. I was wearing boxer shorts and one of Dad's T-shirts, my hair tangled down my back. People always say that you look different in the mirror than in reality, but Rocco looked exactly the same. I kissed him on the cheek.

'No kids,' he said. I walked out of the bathroom and Rocco followed me upstairs to the loft. I sat down on his bed and he sat down on mine. The soldiers were dispersing through the whole house somehow. I picked up my flute and held it like a gun. I pointed one end at him and pretended to shoot, letting myself fall backwards on to the bed as if I'd been pushed.

'What exact time does she go out?' I said, being pedantic and still lying backwards on the bed. I looked at Rocco through my legs, which I hitched up on to the bed and he looked back with a smile.

'Exactly eleven Isabel, I don't know, if we get there early we can play it by ear.' He laughed, running his hand through his long hair and looking at me. 'Are you going to come with me or shall I go by myself?' he asked, and I felt the tight knot in my tummy shudder slightly. I put some black clothes over my pyjamas, then the black coat Rocco had found and then the black hat and gloves. Rocco did the same and as we left through the back door he slung a bag over his shoulder.

Outside we stepped over ice like we were stepping on eggshells and the air came out of our mouths frozen. The sky was moss black and lit by the orange street lamps, making patches of Camden glow and other patches disappear. The snow had been melting and freezing so rapidly recently that it was just a grey ice with a mould of white on the top and the streaks of white still sitting on the drains and the roofs looking like highlighter pen. The ice crunched under

our shoes as we walked hand-in-hand down the
street.

It was about ten-thirty and Camden was buzzing.
All the cold gypsy-dressed people huddled in queues
outside plastic-signed bars where music thumped
from the cheap doors. If we really were going to do
this, which I half-assumed we weren't, we thought it
might perhaps be a good idea to have a drink first, so
we made our way into our local pub on the corner of
the road where we sat silently at the back, drinking
vodka and tonic and distractedly eating peanuts. I
don't know why I even contemplated it. You'll think,
reading this, that I was doing exactly what my brother
told me, and maybe I was, but there was also an
element of interest. A sadness, a love and an interest.
My hair was tied up in a high ponytail that slipped
down my back and I wore some greasy red lipstick.
The background noise was heavy so we didn't try to
fight it with conversation. My elbows felt pointy, my
skin powdery. Rocco was smoking and looking around
the large dark pub. It was crowded with people and
smelt of sweat, candle wax, cigarettes and beer. The
wood of the pub table at the far end was wet with
lemonade and gave off a sappy smell.

Four drunken men were sitting at the table behind
Rocco and it struck me how unattractive they were
compared to my brother. Even in the candle darkness
of the pub, their faces were bloated and contorted. I

studied Rocco's profile, his thick eyebrows hunched up and his olive skin warm and smooth as drum leather. He lifted his cigarette and began to cut the room up with it, hovering it like an artist's pencil and shutting one of his eyes. He focused on a blond girl with stubby legs and big breasts and then moved away, pointing onto a young couple kissing. Then he lifted it between himself and me, watching me sternly until my face broke into a smile.

I was trying to guess how pure people were by their expressions. There were quite a few young people there, which made for a more interesting game even though age isn't necessarily a factor. Rocco perhaps could see I was playing the game, or he started to play of his own accord, because he nodded in the direction of the blond girl he had been eyeing up previously.

'Virgin,' he said, and I raised my eyebrows disbelievingly. She was quite pretty, waving her arms about expressively, and her jeans were so tight around her large bottom that I could see her knicker line. She looked uncomfortable in her clothes, but attractive. I shook my head and shrugged, the noise in the pub gave little margin for normal conversation. I thought that either she slept around and didn't worry about it, or Rocco was right and she was a virgin, because she had an unhurt look in her eyes.

The barman was tall and dark, innocent in the sense that he looked impregnable with his big shoulders and stubble, as if he'd never let himself get hurt, but he'd probably had some pretty dirty sex in his life. He looked violent. There was a couple watching each other, soft as deer. There were a lot of drunk people, whose emotions were clouded by drink so it was difficult to tell. There was a middle-aged man who looked pained, a girl who looked tearful even when she was laughing. The pub was bursting at the seams like a sardine can, and after our quick watchful drink, we walked stonily through the crowded high street to the emptier back streets.

Near the end of the high street, where the crowds thinned to a weak paste, we turned right. I was walking blindly, my head perhaps switched off by adrenaline, but Rocco's hand was comfortingly large over mine. At the end of that street we turned left and Rocco's chosen house came solidly into view. Opposite was a fence and some shrubbery hiding a little square of derelict land behind it. The house was isolated and detached on the corner. The smaller house to its left was positioned away from it and the one on the right not near enough to pose a problem. The BMW we normally saw in the driveway wasn't there and all the lights in the house were off, the windows black. It was the kind of large house that would sport a small, well kept garden full of tulips and rhododendrons. It was a sharp shallow building with two floors, but it had a long body and didn't go back far. The walls were almost as white as the snow and the windows large and dark.

Rocco and I walked confidently round the back, still holding each other's gloved hands. There was a brick wall surrounding the garden, which Rocco gave me a leg over and I slid quiet as a mouse on to the wet turf of the garden. He handed me the bag and then hauled himself gracefully over the wall. It was all a very quiet manoeuvre and I tried not even to breathe because the air around seemed so liquid silent.

It's amazing how different everything looks at night. This house, which was usually so content with its white walls and big welcoming windows, now seemed to be squinting nervously at us. I thought of a haunted house in a children's book with a frown and curved window ledges like eyebrows.

We padded quietly through the little garden towards the house. The shadows distorted the straight lines of the walls and made the house appear slanted. There was a window open a chink at the top, but it was too high to climb. Rocco looked at me and nodded to the largest window, where the panes were so large that I'd be able to fit through without breaking more than one. He took a spare jumper out of his bag and wrapped it around his arm, smashing the glass at the corner so it shattered in tiny pieces like bulky rain around our feet.

I slid right through the square, feeling dumb and

blind as a lizard. The window was close to the floor in the dining room and I rolled delicately on to the shiny hardwood floor. There were obviously no children in this house, the walls were too white and the lines too straight. I guessed the man worked with computers and that they only moved in last year because the floor still had the smell of new varnish and there was a faint damp odor of paint.

I stood up, found keys sitting snug in their holes in the back door, and opened it. Rocco walked into the house, looking around silently. I closed the door and he followed me into the kitchen. I had a weird sensation of being underwater, only able to move very smoothly and only able to communicate by signals. I swam into the kitchen, which was small and neat with white sideboards and a huge buzzing plastic built-in fridge. I couldn't imagine anyone living in this house, with its surgical white plastic cabinets and geo-metrical lines. I gestured upstairs and my brother nodded, following me up on to the second wide, carpeted landing.

I walked through the door opposite the stairs, turning the shiny brass handle with my leather hands. There were keys in all the doors. Inside, the bed was in the middle of the room and there was a light on either side. There were two identical wardrobes facing each other on the walls, both closed and neat. To the left, the door to an ensuite bathroom was slightly open. I heard Rocco go into another room, picking up his feet carefully. I opened the drawer on one side of the bed, which was neat with a book and a pen and a tampon. The drawer on the opposite side had fifty quid in it along with a chequebook and a pad of paper. I pocketed the money. I opened the wardrobe on the man's side of the bed and carefully went through the pockets of each pair of trousers and each jacket. The cash in his trousers mounted up to about fifty pounds again, clumped in five-pound notes and coins.

I walked out of the room, wanting to get out of the house now, full of an uneasy feeling, and losing sight of why we were doing this. Rocco was in the man's study, searching through the drawers and he turned to me with a big grin on his face, holding up a wad of cash. I noted his discovery and gestured that we should go. He lifted up a finger – just a minute – and I hovered in the doorway shifting from foot to foot and feeling suffocated by the silence. My hands began to shake but Rocco looked steady; I was the lizard and he was a cat with eager paws and sharp eyes.

Suddenly, the door downstairs opened and slammed shut again. Rocco perked up, pocketing the money and I looked at him: what should we do? I asked with my eyes. Through the suffocating silence, female bare feet came closer up the stairs. Neither of us moved, he still as a cat and me still as a lizard. There was a long, bell-jar pause.

She walked into the bedroom, leaving the door open, and we heard her sit heavily on the bed. Rocco walked silently out into the hallway and I stood in the doorframe of the study. Without looking at me Rocco closed the door of the bedroom on her and turned the brass key, locking her in. I was shocked by the swiftness of Rocco's cruelty and my features tangled into a scared frown. Rocco shrugged and looked at me.

'Who's there?' the lady said nervously. She sounded about forty, possibly foreign. Rocco and I walked down the stairs as she began to rattle the door. I tried not to listen to her shouting out, banging on the door, and then her high pitched screaming as Rocco and I made our exit through the back and into her garden. To my relief, we couldn't hear her shouts from there, and Rocco hoisted me over the wall quickly before following me himself.

As soon as we hit the pavement we walked briskly around the corner. I was sweating and felt fragile as glass. When we were some way away he held me steady in a hot hug that smelt of sweat and relief.

When we got home, giggles made my head feel light, although I still had this excess of leaden adrenaline in my stomach. I was shaking from the cold and we sat in the messy kitchen and ate the ends from an old Chinese dinner, feeling deflated after the tears and the giggles and the excitement. There was almost nothing else in the fridge but bread, cheese and old rice. We let the mouse crawl across the table between us. I thought about how Rocco and my whole relationship could be traced through the pretty scars on our skin. I ran my fingers over the scar on my wrist from falling off the swing, and stared at the scar across Rocco's slanted nose created by me the first time I lost my temper.

'What?' Rocco said gruffly when he saw me staring at him.

'Just looking,' I said.

'At what?' he replied, pushing away the box of cold rice.

'Nothing,' I said.

'What?' he said.

'Nothing!' I laughed.

There was another pause as we resumed eating. I got up and closed the curtains in the kitchen. We didn't talk about what we'd just done, but I felt child-like with exhilaration. Perhaps young people are only vulnerable to getting older. We're vulnerable to being filled up with horrible things into our milky brains. I thought of the woman screaming. When you're a kid you're not one thing, you are everything and, potentially, even more. You play families and you can be mummy or baby depending on your mood. You choose to be the firewoman and in your head you are the firewoman. Then something happens, some first time, perhaps you see a fire engine and it makes you jump. Consciously it doesn't make much of an impression, but subconsciously you know you're not going to be a fireman anymore. You solidify a little, congeal a little.

Rocco put his hand over my hand. 'You're hot,' he said, and I shrugged. I wanted to bite something. I wished that I'd never met Jackson, certainly that I'd never slept with him. I kept having split-second visionary memories while doing unrelated things, like him inside me and not looking at me. Later, sitting in this smoky hostel room, looking out on the rubbish filled alleyway and sitting on our unmade bed, Rocco asked me if I ever loved Jackson and I said no, I never loved Jackson. I slept with him and I enjoyed sleeping with him and I'm glad I slept with him, but I didn't love him. Then he hurt me and it was such a relief that I had never loved him.

I shrugged and took off my jumper, holding my hair away from my hot neck and wiping the sweat before letting my hair drop back.

'What does the outside man want?' I asked Rocco nervously, snapping the cheap wooden chopsticks across each other at their greasy ends. 'What does everyone want?' I stuck the sticks in the box of rice and Rocco smiled at me like I was a child. The lighting was very dim as each of the light bulbs in the kitchen sporadically burst and we were left with only one naked bulb trying desperately to light the whole room. I laughed through the tightness in my throat and began to plait my hair, folding the clumps over each other comfortingly. As soon as I let go it all unwound again. There was grease on my fingers and by mistake I wiped it on the ends of my hair, making the auburn colour darken and shine. Rocco smiled as he leant over the kitchen table to kiss my forehead.

—⁂—

18

THE LANDLORD

While Rocco had his mouth on my forehead, I saw someone at the door of the kitchen and my heart jumped, picking up speed again as I broke away from my brother and stared cat-eyed at the door. I thought for a lovely moment that Dad might have come home and I imagined him well again, happy and glowing, walking in as if nothing had happened. It was not Dad, but the landlord with the hooked nose and slipping face. My heart beat faster.

'Hello again,' the man said in his slow voice, taking a step inside our dank kitchen. I remembered insect senses and tried to smell what the man was thinking, but all I could taste was darkness and damp. I cupped my hands and held the mouse on my lap, stroking its little ears. We stared at him.

'How the hell did you get in?' said Rocco.

'I've been looking around the house. What a mess!' He half-smiled and rubbed his big nose. I thought of the puddles of water in the hall, the smell of Chinese food, the mouldy pizza boxes, our mouse, and old newspapers over the kitchen. The yellow walls which Mum used to say reminded her of sunny days were now tinted an even sicker yellow by Rocco's cigarettes, the floors were burnt by the butts and the ornamental plates in the sitting room were covered in ash. There were dead moths in the curtains, dust on the mantelpieces and the plants were disintegrating. The man looked sinister and droopy in the doorway, like a frog from a bedtime story.

'How did you get in the house?' Rocco repeated loudly.

The man paused to scratch his shoulder for a moment while Rocco and I sat very still.

'With a key,' he said, as if he was stating the obvious. 'Has your mother not explained the arrangements to you?'

'No.' Rocco said quietly. 'We haven't spoken to Mum or Dad.'

The landlord sighed. 'Your parents have borrowed a fair amount of money from me, that antique shop is hardly a gold mine, and recently they haven't been paying rent. What with interest and such, it's a good sum of money they owe. So I found them.'

I looked up at this hook-noosed, ash-skinned man standing in our kitchen holding a coffee cup and felt appalled. My mouth was dry, with a acidic taste creeping over my tongue.

'They don't tell you much, do they? Hey ho,' he said. 'They sold me the house, as they're going to be away for a while.'

I swallowed hard and it hurt my throat.

'They would have told us,' I said meekly, thinking that things could not have got that bad. 'They love this house.'

'Your mother hates this house,' the landlord informed us. 'Is it very cold in here? I suppose you kids couldn't pay the heating bill. Never mind,' he said condescendingly. 'Do you mind if I make myself some tea?'

He moved to the kettle and flicked the switch, which made a buzzing sound that was usually comforting, but now sounded like locusts.

'Here's the deal,' the landlord said, blinking his padded eyelids over his damp eyes. 'I'm making the house into flats and I bought it on the grounds that I keep the loft intact and let you stay there for a reduced rate. I assume you both have jobs or something. Mummy and Daddy haven't entirely forgotten about the little ones.' He hardly opened his lips when he spoke, and I wondered if he was hiding a vast sticky tongue in his hot mouth. I was painfully aware of his presence and my hatred for this betrayed house. The damp was rising up the paper walls, the origami paper wrinkling and wilting.

The man took some crumpled pieces of paper from his shoulder bag, which he had put on the floor, and he placed them in front of Rocco and me with a slow flourish. They were the deeds to the house, with Mum's neat signature on the dotted line at the bottom showing that our house now belonged to the melting man. I touched the signature with my fingers as the man poured himself a mug of tea and leant on the sideboard.

'You've let the house fall apart,' the man said to us. 'There's damp and the plumbing's shot, but we can hide all that. I think it will make nice flats.'

'I don't believe this,' I said as the man sipped the hot tea carefully, trying not to burn his big tongue.

'I only saw your mother.'

'Where are they? Why hasn't she contacted us?'

The landlord shrugged. 'I don't know. I'm not a family man. All I know is that she isn't coming home to this house and that's all that concerns me. Work isn't going to start here for another two weeks, so you have time to pack everything up, all the antiques and furniture are mine, but you can keep the loft as it stands. By the time I see you next I want this hallway to be full of boxes, no questions asked.'

'Fine,' Rocco said.

'Good,' he said. 'I'm glad we've got this over with, I'll see you in two weeks.'

After Dad's landlord closed the front door, I felt my first real hatred. I'd never hated Mum or Dad, although at points I thought I did, but this damaging boulder ache was deeper than any dislike I'd felt before. It was a sick heavy feeling like a lingering food poisoning in my stomach.

I still remember running into the kitchen after school one day when I was eight, eyes jumping with a desperate inspiration because Rocco and I had seen a slug of oil moving across a puddle as if it was alive and were amazed by it. The puddle was marshy and the oil a trembling locket on top, sliding in the shape of a lizard. Rocco and I stopped, transfixed by the colours, and Rocco grabbed a stick to poke it with, but when he touched it the skin shuddered and split. The colours dispersed and changed, the shapes clinging to the water in an energetic, excited way.

This was the first time we had seen oil with water and it seems silly now to be so amazed by the spillage from a broken car and although perhaps it wasn't the most influential first time – it wasn't sex or love – it had a certain charm. Oil is only unromantic because older people know how it is made and what it is. When what you see in oil is liquid and colour, it's pretty as fire or some kinky Ingres painting. Oil and mud are a child's form of sex, disgusting and compelling at the same time.

Dad was the only person home when we let ourselves into the hallway, gabbling about the sticky, coloured animal living in the puddle. He stood above us and instructed us to speak slowly, smiling the same lovely grin that Rocco has now, before deciding to give us a chemistry lesson. We sat in the yellow kitchen looking up at our Dad, who was wearing green tweed trousers and a checked woollen jumper. In those days he was much more together. He got a glass of water and put gun oil in it, so the oil separated into lively floating marbles on the surface. Then he explained to us how millions of years ago animals in the sea died and fell to the bottom of the ocean. Then more animals covered these animals and the bottom layer was eventually crushed to this amazing thick, grey pulp called oil. He went on about the different types of oils, the hydrocarbons, the methods of distillation, but we engrossed ourselves in playing with the oil. Perhaps Rocco understood Dad's explanation, but I certainly couldn't get my head around the idea that there were crushed animals inside the heavy liquid. The closest I got was the thought that perhaps there were tiny bugs trapped under the skin and they made the flesh wobble, so I retained my innocent awe. Rocco was always far more intelligent than I was and I have to say that from the beginning I never got joy from facts. They were like a wall, refusing to let clouds be clouds and trees be trees.

'I want to take things from Jackson's house,' I said to Rocco as we sat in the quiet, the landlord's tea still sitting hot and only half drunk on our counter.

'His mother goes to an evening art class on Saturday nights, doesn't she?' Rocco said. 'And Jackson will be out somewhere.' He began to fiddle with the plastic casing of his cigarette packet, slipping it away from the cardboard and lighting the edge of it with his lighter. The whole thing folded suddenly in on itself, almost disappearing and releasing a rancid smell like the smell of burning hair. The grey smoke tumbled up around the dark kitchen and I could taste the smell in my mouth.

20

AFFAIRS AND DRUG ADDICTED OLD PEOPLE

Paris is full of piano music, something I've never liked. I can play the piano, but I always get the feeling that the hollow notes don't mesh together, only igniting for a moment and then giving themselves up to the sound of another one, while with the flute everything jumps and falls together. Dad used to like piano music and he'd sit at the kitchen table in the evening reading the papers and listening to Bach. He would spend hours reading the papers, not just skimming the headlines and reading a few articles like most people, but actually concentrating on every article, underlining sentences and ripping pieces out to put in his messy collection of cuttings. Sometimes I read the bits he cut out and they were always things about historical misinformation and they bored me.

Rocco hates me writing this book, he's always saying that I never play my flute anymore, but of course I don't, I left it in London sitting on the bedcover creases with the limping pigeon and the rest of the toy soldiers. I wish I could explain to him the difference between music and words that bothers me. Dad once told me about a philosopher before Socrates who got it into his head that the world was made of opposites which, when they rubbed up against each other, in effect caused existence. He was famous for the words, 'The world is in continual flux.' Light is sure, so is darkness, but dawn is better because it is the friction of opposites. All of the world is continually changing and nothing is ever the same from one second to the next.

Music is beautiful because it sums up that movement and energy that makes the world, opposite notes and all the bits in between coming together to make a pretty tune, but words are beautiful because they are rare solid things. They can be rhythmic, or charming, or boring, but they are mostly firm. I couldn't describe what happened to us in London with a flute under my breath or ivory notes under my fingers, but I can document it in these lovely straight lines. Codivi wrote, 'The principle of time which consumes everything,' but it doesn't consume words. Words consume time and trap it within some reasonable framework. Time scares me. Rocco doesn't want it to jump backwards or forwards or to stand still or to turn itself inside out, but is fine with it continuing its little steps forward.

I have to keep these papers with me all the time at the moment. I take them with me to the café and keep them under the bed when we're in our room because Rocco is beginning to hate these words so much that I think he might try and throw them away. I'd leave him if he did that, at least for a while to teach him a lesson. He hit me yesterday too, an example of how he's beginning to get more violent since we left London. I don't think he really meant to, it was just a slap, but it shook me, because it was exactly what Dad might have done if Mum had sworn at him.

I remember when, after Dad began to get more skeletal and tired, Mum began arguing more and Rocco and I listened to our parents from outside their bedroom door. Two little Iagos, we turned up the heating in the house to make them more flustered. We were angry with both of them for having ignored us for the last two weeks and the heating was our secret revenge, turning the house into a sauna.

'But why not?' Mum said loudly.

I shrugged, looking with bewilderment at my brother, who was hunched up in a hot ball with his ear strained to the door.

I could imagine Dad's thin mouth frowning limply,

his body sharp and all his thin limbs pointy. Mum was starting to cry now, the heat sliming around all of us, a corrosive damp collecting.

'The answer is simply no,' he said. I could imagine Dad's face close to Mum's, his hot breath on her soft red cheeks.

'But why?' she said breathily.

'Is it hot?' Dad said. 'It's those bloody children playing with the thermostat. God damn it, Kate, we used to have such a good time.'

There was a pause and Rocco and I wondered what was going on until we heard ugly squelching noises, gasps and creaks, and we scuttled upstairs to let them roast in their own sweat.

I thought of that evening, that insane heat, because with the heating off in the house Rocco and I were getting terribly cold. We didn't really want to waste our money on boring bills – perhaps we had a feeling that we would need it for something more important soon, so instead we chose to freeze.

Jackson's house was a lot like our house, a semi-detached, white-painted, small-windowed, three-storey house in one of the streets off Camden High Street. It had a small garden like ours, but it was neater than our house.

I don't know why we did this.

All the lights were off in the windows and we mounted the fence surrounding the garden, softly just like before. It was earlier in the evening and Jackson's house is closer to other houses. It is on the end of a row, so it was easy to get into the back garden, but we had to be careful because there were people walking the streets every so often. We got over the wall without anyone seeing and crouched to catch our breath behind a bush at the back of the rectangular garden. At the back of the garden were some shrubs with a white picnic table and chairs near the front. One of the chairs had been blown over in the strong winter wind and the snow on the plants made my bottom damp. When my legs began to ache from crouching, we raised ourselves nervously and silently looked at Jackson's house. We'd seen it in the dark before, but never with this much adrenaline-induced clarity.

We walked towards the house at the edge of the garden where the shadows were the densest. We were wearing gloves, heavy black jackets and hats just like last time. This time, instead of breaking a window and making that loud shattering sound, Rocco took a coat hanger out of his bag and a bit of plastic. He had a knack with locks and in less than a minute we were in Jackson's little hallway.

This time, entering the house, there was no floating feeling of being somewhere we didn't know. I had been here a million times before, I'd even snuck in here at night with Jackson when we'd broken his curfew. It had a different atmosphere now and Rocco and I listened for any human sound, but heard nothing. We didn't know it, but Jackson's grandfather was dozing at the very top of the house listening for his daughter to shout that she had come home from her art class early. Of course she didn't.

Rocco and I climbed the carpeted stairs up to the first landing and knew just where to go for money. We went first to a cupboard in his mother's bedroom where Jackson used to take loose change from. I opened it and scooped a pile of notes and shiny coins into Rocco's bag, not knowing quite how much there was. We went through her drawers, picking up money here and there and, as some of it clinked together we lifted our heads, thinking we heard something upstairs. We paused, but all there was was silence.

I left his mother's floral bedroom and walked through the dark hallway towards Jackson's bedroom door. I looked back at Rocco, who nodded at me, but I didn't move so Rocco placed his hand over mine on the cool doorknob and turned it for me. I turned my head to him as his hands moved mine and felt his hot breath on my lips close to his. We both walked into the small room. It looked out over the street and all the pasty-lit walls were plastered with posters of bands. There was a rock group dressed in black and their grave charcoal encrusted eyes watched me solemnly as I went over to Jackson's desk. There were pages of magazines also tacked on to the wall, a blonde girl lying on the bonnet of a shiny red car wearing red knickers and covering her breasts with her hands and their red-painted nails, a female pop star in cut-off jean shorts and a bikini top, and a set of song lyrics from a CD case. He had some school books piled on his desk and a pad of file paper with the beginning of a doodle in blue ink. A couple of biro pens sat on Jackson's dresser and it was fairly neat. All his drawers were closed, the floors were clean and everything was arranged in piles except for a few CD's on the floor, detached from their cases. It was very hot and silent in the room. Inside his wardrobe were clothes, lined up on their wire hangers in an orderly way, and with quiet ceremony, I used Jackson's Swiss Army knife to carefully cut down the material of his shirts and the legs of his trousers while Rocco snapped all the CDs, one after the other.

Then I opened Jackson's desk drawers and inside was exactly what I expected, a large amount of weed and a rock wrapped in separate pieces of cling film. There were also two packs of cigarettes, three lighters, a tall bottle of vodka and a little herb bag with what looked like magic mushrooms. Rocco smiled at me and I picked up Jackson's stash, carried it out into the hallway and then into his mother's room, where I dumped it all in the middle of her bed.

Jackson was very conscientious about not letting his doting mother find out that he did drugs, because she had a low-tolerance American-high-school-prom-queen view on life. Just as I dropped the stuff with a clatter on to the bed, both Rocco and I heard steps in the house for sure. I held my breath and stopped dead. There was the sound of creaking again, the weighty groan of a floorboard stepped on heavily and slowly. Rocco and I shot each other another look and heard sirens in the distance.

We went out into the hallway nervous and apprehensive. The sirens were getting closer and my heart beat faster, its pace picking up as the yawning siren vibrated nearer.

'There are always sirens in Camden,' Rocco whispered. 'Don't look so nervous.' I looked up the staircase that led to the third floor and saw the tall shadow of a man hiding at the top. The man shifted from foot to foot at the top of the stairs and the sound of the creaking floor sounded loud in the quiet. He took a step forward and then saw us standing at the base of the stairs and stood back again.

The siren was so close now, but I couldn't move. It was like my body had been filled up with some stiff heavy metal. My limbs wouldn't move and I felt useless. I wanted to get out of the house, but felt frozen. Then Rocco burst into action and grabbed my hand, almost dragging me to the nearest window, which he opened as wide as he could, setting off the house alarm loud in our ears. It was the window in the hallway and it was one floor down to the garden.

'Isabel, the sirens aren't for us,' I heard him say. 'There are always sirens in Camden, you know that.'

I looked worried.

'I promise they're not,' he whispered, squeezing my hand. My body still felt heavy, but I forced myself to move. Rocco dropped the bag and it landed with a thud on the grass in front of the patio. Rocco got out of the window first and grabbed on to the cold metal drainpipe. I watched his face, which was glowing as he slid down, his mouth set in almost a grin of interest and his eyes bright. He hugged the drain and it didn't look all that hard. Rocco didn't exactly do it gracefully, he scrambled with his hands against the metal to try and steady himself against the joins and his legs hung unsteadily from his body. The metal was wet with ice, the sirens became unbearably near, as Rocco watched me climb out the window. I began my descent in a similar way to Rocco, not graceful but bearable. I found it was easiest when I lodged my feet against the joins and squeezed really hard over the frosty metal. The noise of the sirens filled up all the space around me and I suddenly fell the last bit on to the grass, landing in a heap, shaken but not hurt and my hands covered with rash from the rusting metal. The siren was on Jackson's street now and Rocco and I lost no time in scrambling chaotically over the fence. I was breathing cold air faster then I've ever breathed in my life and had what felt like pure adrenaline spinning in my clenched arteries.

Just as I had steadied myself, legs feeling soft as air, I turned my head and saw Jackson walking quickly towards us through the straight dark street. He was just a shadow even when he was only a few feet in front of us, but his particular walk, with hunched shoulder and thin build made it impossible that it was just a passing stranger. My eyes, accustomed to the dark now, matched his stare and there was a heavy, empty pause where nothing in London seemed to breathe except the wheezing siren. I blinked and he didn't, just staring at us like a rabbit caught in the headlights. It wouldn't have surprised me if all of our hearts had been beating in time for that brief moment as the siren got clearer in the black Camden streets. There was a certain look in his eyes, perhaps just shock, but possibly a look that was trying to persuade himself that he could somehow manage to ignore the two figures standing oddly outside his house. The look only lasted a second and then I felt Rocco move off behind me and I lingered for one extra sight of Jackson's eyes, trying to read his shadowed expression before turning and following Rocco as Jackson legged it into his house. Quick and scared, Rocco and I disappeared into Camden and lost ourselves in the back streets.

—⚏—

21

BURGLARY

The wonderful thing about cities is that you can't see the balance of opposites through the jumble and chaos, but echoes are there all the same. Concrete jarring against the trees, trees repeating down the street. Pavement slabs the same everywhere, modern buildings copying each other. When we arrived home, echo and balance being what it is even in unbalanced cities, someone had been in our house. We guessed that it was someone working for the landlord, because everything stolen was valuable. He obviously didn't trust us to pack up like we'd been told to. The water in the hallway, which had formed an almost perfect oval as it fell through the floor, had been splashed around by boots walking through it. The scabbing bubbles were broken and there was water on the walls.

One of the big metal guns was still sitting on the

side table, just to the right of the door, perhaps not thought to be worth any money. In the sitting room the magazines and books were on the floor and the sofa was on its side, a clock face smashed, some of the ink pots broken on the floor. A picture had been taken down, the frame broken at one of the corners, and the mirror where Rocco had made me take off my make-up that time was face down on the carpet. Quite a few of the more valuable looking small antiques that Mum and Dad kept in the sitting room were gone now. In the kitchen, the contents of the table had been swept on to the floor, the drawers left open and gushing. Our silver cutlery was gone, as was one of our VCRs.

Upstairs in Mum and Dad's room they had been through every little thing, and I wondered sadly what they might have found. It looked like clothes, mostly the newer of Dad's suits, had been taken. Even the loft was upside down and shaken, our soldiers almost stifled under an avalanche of debris. The windows were open and the messy papers lifted and shifted with each snowy and freezing breath. A bit of money from my bedside table had been taken and both of our purses, with our address books and bank cards included – not that they'd get much money out of that. We'd hidden our money behind the fridge in the kitchen and they hadn't got it.

I can't say exactly what I thought as I looked at all this, I don't remember. The big pigeon who had taken

up residence in the chimney next to the balcony
seemed to have flown in and was sitting contentedly
in the folds of Rocco's bed. He looked at us with his
bubble eyes when we came in – telling us to bugger
off.

The pigeon got bored of our stagnant figures
standing near the door and turned his feathery neck
back to the folds of the duvet, shuffling slightly. I
wondered what pigeon flesh looked like under that
pavement slab grey; probably pink, I thought.

Rocco slid his back down against the wall so that he
was crouching near the floor, his head back and his
eyes closed with exasperation. He put our bag down
next to him, on top of some papers.

'Right,' I said slowly, and Rocco laughed half-
heartedly from under his hands, which were sup-
porting his head. I walked into the twisted room,
stepping between a jumble of clothes and books. In
the corner, the shoebox of moths had been opened
and tipped slightly on its side so that the bodies had
skidded from their careful places. I knelt down and
picked each furry body up with my cold fingers,
placing half of them in the bottom of the shoe box and
half of them in the lid. They were grey, and almost
parchment yellow and their leafy wings looked see-
through and ancient. I touched them very softly so
that they wouldn't crack under my fingers and I felt
their fine powder gather itself on my skin. I smoothed

out the wrinkles in the sheet of my bed, the one the pigeon hadn't made its nest on, and I lifted the moths and their cardboard trays up on to it, away from the floor clutter. The mouse was still safe in her cage, and I took her out, placing her in my pocket where her little nose just crept above the material.

'Do you think we have any pins in this house?' I said to Rocco, not feeling like analysing the events of the last couple of hours. I took my hat off and ran mothy fingers through my hair. I picked up a band from the floor and began to put all the long auburn strands in a high ponytail near the top of my head to keep it away from the sweaty back of my neck. The tail slunk over my shoulder and I shivered slightly.

'Probably,' Rocco said.

I looked at the moths, then I turned and looked at Rocco, who was watching me with his big, mournful kitten eyes. He had his hands in his hair so that the dark curls were sticking out from between his pale fingers.

Rocco took out of his pocket the four soldiers we had promoted to general that rainy day when we had stolen the soldiers from Dad's derelict shop, and he let them look at their struggling army fighting their way from under our clothes. He put them back in his pocket while I picked up the two trays of insects and walked over to the door.

'Let's go find some pins,' I said, and Rocco picked

up the bag with the money in it and followed me down the staircase. The landing outside Mum and Dad's room had layers of faint odors of dampness, cigarettes, hash and a slight smell of Chinese food from downstairs, but underneath all this I thought I could still smell Mum's floral perfume trying to escape the stranglehold of the rest. The cardboard felt fake under my fingers and my nose was cold.

'Did you bring my hat down?' I asked Rocco and he lifted up the black woollen hat from the bag with a nod. 'It's so cold,' I said, and he looked worried for a moment. I wound my way around the water's crusty bubbles into the sitting room, while Rocco went to get some pins. In the sitting room, I put the moths down on the empty coffee table in the middle of the room so that I could put the sofa back up and look around for something that I could mount the moths on with the pins. I picked up the painting of the Virgin Mary with a cracked frame and turned it around to see if the board behind was soft. I remembered Mum and Dad telling me about this picture, taken from an altarpiece somewhere and painted on wood. The front was ugly, a modern painter creating something in half-hearted high-gothic style. The Virgin was sitting on an architectural throne, her face blank with a three-quarter stare out into space, and she was showing off this tiny little wrinkled man sitting on her lap. She had a moth-coloured face, the shape of an almond with a tight mouth and flat nose. I took the frame off with a satisfying crack of splintering wood, leaving only the sharp-edged piece of tanned modern wood, the kind with grains all the same size. Mum and Dad weren't religious, so I didn't really understand the need for the ugly little painting. I turned the wood over to look at the painting again. I could understand, in a way, why people were religious. The painting did have a kind of calming quality, the kind of calm that parents evoke when you're very young and see them outside the school gates and the kind of calm Rocco sometimes makes me feel now.

Rocco came in with a plastic box of pins and put them down on the coffee table with two cups of tea, before sitting on the newly stabilised sofa. He turned on the remaining television and flipped through the channels so that a jumpy blue light fled into the room. I took the board over to the table and arranged it next to the trays of moths, kneeling on the floor under it. I placed the first, biggest moth with large taut wings gently on my palm and nudged it on to the centre of the board. Carefully I took one of the pins and let the sharp end slide into the furry tummy of the moth's body and then into the soft wood. I did the same thing with the rest of the moths that were still intact, so that they made a pretty pattern on the wood, secure now and organised.

I wasn't all that interested in stuff being structured

at the beginning of all this. Rocco was the one with the ordered head. But when stuff begins to turn to slight, furtive chaos around you, perhaps you look for more categorised solids in your head and vision. As I've said, that is what these words are. In a way Rocco has become less interested in not being part of disarray since we left London because he refuses to organise his memories, but instead occupies himself with forgetting them. Forgetting Mum's face, forgetting her frowns, her slow voice, Dad's smoker's cough rumbling through the house at night, his milky eyes. I don't want to forget them, I just want the memories to be organised, so that after a while I can begin to ignore them. One day, I want to live in a little farm house where you don't have to look for echoes and balance in your surroundings, because they're obvious from every angle. I'll have dogs and cats and chickens and donkeys and a little bedroom with a low wooden roof, which will look out over a blank horizon. My birthday was going to sneak up on me three weeks from that evening, which was strange, because if my head was becoming more interested in organised solids, perhaps I was losing all that slippery childhood innocence. I always somehow felt that I'd stay sixteen for ever, but since time was suddenly passing very quickly, this obviously wasn't going to turn out to be so.

'Should we call the police?' I said.

'In the circumstances, that wouldn't be wise. It's the

landlord's stuff. He can take it in whatever manner he chooses,' Rocco said.

'Oh,' I said, wishing Mum and Dad were here with us.

I came and sat between Rocco's legs on the sofa, leaning back against him to watch the penguins on television waddle and slide into the frothy water while Rocco lit up a cigarette. We sat there for a while not speaking. Rocco smoked, putting the cigarette in my mouth from time to time to let me have a drag. The picture was a little fuzzy, as if it was at the end of its energy, and the room, although messy, was very, very still and frozen around us. Only the trees were shivering outside our window and the television penguins wobbling. I didn't remember having eaten for ages, but I wasn't at all hungry.

Loud in the hush of the house as we watched the silent television, there was a knock at the door and we got up from the sofa. I went out into the damp yellow hall as Rocco lagged behind slightly, still standing at the door of the sitting room with his bare feet while I looked through the peephole at my ex-boyfriend pounding on the door. He was smashing on it hard and my heart jumped up, making me feel sick. He was wearing a black jumper and his neck stuck up sharply from its triangular collar, the muscles jutting away from the bones. His blue eyes were wider than usual, trapping all the different shades of shadow into them like a monochrome prism.

'Jackson,' I mouthed at Rocco through the broken quiet.

Jackson pounded again and shouted something, I forget what, but his mouth was huge and puckered from my distorted peephole viewpoint. I looked back and Rocco shrugged lightly.

'Go away,' I called to Jackson, but Rocco mouthed that I should let him in, tilting his head to the side and frowning as if he were trying to remember something from a long time ago.

'We need to talk,' Jackson shouted roughly. He stopped the pounding on the door and I tentatively removed the bolt and opened it. I looked nervously at him while my hand shook against the wall, but he didn't catch my eye, instead pushing past me towards Rocco so that they were standing almost opposite each other in the yellow hallway. There was one of my shoes in the middle of the puddle, to the front left of where Jackson was standing and the old metal gun was on the sideboard next to a can of diet Coke to his right. I ran my finger along the jutting frieze of the room, dislodging dust on to my finger, watching Rocco's almost amused face.

Rocco had an annoying habit of looking vaguely ironic whenever somebody was about to get angry. If I got angry with Rocco, he would just let me rant and scream at him, keeping this steady half smile on his face and watching my eyes as they darted. Jackson's face was turning burgundy, perhaps from the cold outside, or perhaps from temper, and Rocco was leaning on the door, smoking a cigarette.

'How are your parents doing?' Rocco said to Jackson, tapping ash onto the floor which fizzed with the heat crushing against the cold water. 'We didn't mean any serious harm, you know.'

'They're a little put out,' Jackson said. 'How are your parents doing?' The voices seemed very loud in the dark origami house.

Rocco shrugged, 'Not really sure, are we Isabel?' He looked at me, mock-plaintively. I could feel my heart beat close under my skin, and I dug my fingernails into the back of my arm, fidgeting with all my limbs as if they were mice crawling against each other. The real mouse was watching calmly from my pocket. My bare feet were cold on the clammy floor and I couldn't seem to blink, making my eyes dry.

'Has your Dad got over his awkward little illness?' Jackson spat at Rocco.

I frowned and I could see Rocco's confident half-smile slip for a moment before regaining its fake composure.

'It's not easy having Aids,' Jackson smiled at Rocco.

Rocco's hand slipped behind to the side of his body, where it hung and he raised his eyebrows slowly so that the lines of his forehead fanned up. I caught my breath and lifted my chin slightly, my body feeling suddenly blank as if it had been drained. I put a hand on the sideboard to steady myself, closing my eyes for a moment.

Until now the tone of their voices had been quite low, as if they were part of the quiet walls of the house, but the next comments were higher pitched, the two of them winding each other up like Jack-in-the-box toys. You wind and wind, childish heart beating in time with the little clicking noise of the box, until the clown bounces out and makes you jump backwards. It wasn't Rocco, but Jackson provoking, so perhaps that had been the case last time too.

'Everybody knows, my parents told me,' Jackson said, louder, his face even redder than it had been when he came in and Rocco's much whiter, showing his disgust.

'Perhaps that explains your perverted morals,' Jackson said.

The water was tickling the skin between my toes and I wiped my feet against the trouser leg, balancing myself against the wall and hardly breathing because it felt like they were using up all the oxygen, creating a vacuum in the hallway.

They stood much firmer on their feet than Mum and Dad used to do when they argued in the house. Mum and Dad had always looked like bugs in a solid cage, while Rocco and Jackson were solid and stern, eyes locked ironically against each other. Rocco was much stronger than Jackson who, although tall, had spindly thin arms and legs. However Jackson looked much more angry and volatile, his hard eyes squinting at my brother. I felt like a catalyst in one of those experiments we used to do in chemistry lessons, standing in the corner holding the mouse in my pocket.

There was a long, tight pause and Rocco dropped his cigarette into the water and rolled up the sleeves of his shirt. Neither of them moved and the air was stagnant and heavy around them, almost marshy and quite suffocating. 'Sleeping with you put her off sex for life,' Rocco laughed at Jackson. 'You must be very proud.'

'She's hardly a great catch, she fucks her own brother.'

'Not true,' Rocco said.

Jackson's eyes widened, his whole face stretching, and he turned to look at me for a second, but he didn't catch my eye and I saw him glance at the gun on the table. While Jackson was turned for half a second, Rocco took a step forward, just a little step, not actually meaning to shock Jackson, but the restraint in Jackson's long, elastic body broke under that little movement and he moved backwards. Then Jackson looked embarrassed at having been so easily caught off guard and without warning, except in the hot expression of his coloured face, he grabbed the metal gun off the sideboard, holding it by the neck like a rock and lunged forcefully at my brother while I blinked. Rocco threw up his hands to protect his head, but the weight of the gun rammed hard against his shoulder, making a cracking sound.

Rocco was only momentarily fazed, but still not actually angry. His emotions were as controlled as his movements and the two boys struggled against each other, both of their hands on the cold flesh of the silver gun and Rocco's shoulder bleeding down his creased white shirt, the colour making veins between the tiny machine stitching. I imagined that the cha-cha was playing mischievously in my head.

They leaned first to the right, both of their hands wrapped tightly around the gun, and they seemed to be almost the same strength as they pushed up against each other, Rocco trying to get Jackson off him, Jackson trying to hit Rocco again. Rocco was forced back a step, right into the doorway of the sitting room, which the two of them filled up. Then Jackson's hand, which was perhaps sweaty with effort, lost its spidery grip on the silver gun and it fell with a panicky jump and a clatter on to the wooden floor, but they didn't stop. It was strange, but they were hardly moving, only locked together in the way arms are often totally still during an arm wrestle.

After Jackson dropped the gun, there was a slight shuffle and Rocco seemed to untangle his hands a little and managed to get a clasp on Jackson's bony shoulders, pushing him off his body with a sudden burst of effort. My hands jumped to my mouth as Jackson lost his balance and was flung backwards, the heels of his feet tripping against one of my shoes in the middle of the floor and sliding forwards on the wet wood. His feet kicked up and his back landed down on the floor, his head smashing with a splash, drenching the house suddenly in very pure silence.

—ᴠᴠᴠ—

Boys

Like a house of leaves, I thought the walls might jump away from the force of Jackson's fall, but before it did I wanted to get upstairs to Mum and Dad's room, so I ran. The rooms used to be able to steadily hold arguments and the sweaty pounding of bodies in beds. It stayed up while being infused with the chemistry of first times, through the blast of last times, but now in the quiet where there was nothing but the moment without a past, it was vulnerable as wrinkling leaves shivering in layers away over my head.

Rocco followed my tantrum up the stairs, two steps at a time, and I opened the wardrobe, kicking clothes out with my wet feet and scrambling my fingers against the shoes, opening boxes and flinging them back, seeing everything in bright colours, but there was nothing. I turned to look at Rocco panting in the doorway.

'It was pills, Izzie,' he said. 'Stuff with long names, Alitretinion, Kaletra, pills to try and stop HIV-related stuff. I'm so sorry. I threw them away. God, I should have said. I'm so sorry.'

'Fuck you, Rocco,' I shouted. He looked angry, flushed and horrible. 'Fuck you! I don't believe you didn't tell me. I don't believe you didn't, shit,' I cried, picking up a stiletto heel from the bed and launching it at him like I did when we were younger while the mouse jumped out of my pocket to watch from the bed. The shoe missed Rocco by a long way this time and only made a dent in Mum and Dad's yellow wallpaper. We both blinked at the same time and I sat down abruptly on the mangled bed. I stared at the room, my hot hands hanging down by my side as if my fingers were sweat off my palms. For a bleary moment I considered leaving him there in the house to find his own way out through what had started to feel like a shifting space, the kind of corridor you'd expect to mutate as you walked through it in your head at night. All of Mum and Dad's stuff were chaotic deposits of padding, her dresses, his books, his ashtray, her earrings, but they didn't make the room any warmer. Nothing in there was remotely maternal or comforting, but all disquiet and agitated possessions, separate, together, painful, a wrongly put together formula.

Instead, I ran downstairs again to see the boy in the doorway of our sitting room. Jackson was very still, his head rolled to one side, his arms limp and his hands still clenched in a fist.

'I'm sorry Isabel, you know it wasn't a conscious decision not to tell you,' Rocco said as he came down the stairs. 'It was just instinct to put something bad away from sight. It's why they've stayed away. He's sick, really sick. He's had expensive treatment abroad, which is why they have no money. Now he's in a special hospital.' Rocco paused, looking up at me, 'Mum agreed that there was no reason to scare you.'

My breathing began to regulate as I watched Jackson's disjointed pale breathing. I inhaled very deeply, my shoulders rising and falling, my eyelids closing for a moment so that all I saw were flicks of light dancing against the black back of my eyelids, moving jaggedly from left to right.

I ran my hands through my hair, looking at Rocco's swollen shoulder tinted with blood and his heavy eyes. I didn't have the strength of character to leave with him watching me. I imagined leaving, knowing he'd let me take half of the money, but I just took another deep breath, still angry, but without the power to decipher all of the reasons, certainly not to articulate them. 'Will Jackson be all right?' I asked.

I wanted to call an ambulance, because even when Jackson came round he seemed delirious and there was a fine trickle of hot blood dribbling from the back of his head, but Rocco frowned at me and shook his head.

'He'll be fine. I doubt we should get anyone else involved, let's keep him here till he's better and then apologise for everything, maybe he won't even make a scene,' he said, as I looked at Jackson's body.

Outside the window, morning was just breaking over the street like egg yolk and we moved Jackson through the watery hall into the sitting room, laying him down on the sofa, where I put pillows behind his head that soaked up the blood from his cut. His face had turned from red to white as we moved him and his neck lolled slightly to the side, his eyes not open, but his breathing heavy and regular. I put a duvet from upstairs over him and sat on the floor next to the sofa with a roll of kitchen towel, shifting his head every so often to try and stop the thick blood. Rocco got out one of his medical text books, pushing aside the board of moths on the coffee table and carefully leafing through the pages to find one on concussion.

'Isabel, stop moving his head,' Rocco said and I stopped mopping up the blood, letting it soak into the pillows and fan out in tiny burgundy streets on either side, clotting in his blond hair. His whole face looked very stern and still, his mouth open and his chest rising and falling peacefully. I put my hand on his smooth forehead, but he was neither particularly cold nor particularly hot, so I let my arm fall back down to the floor and turned to face Rocco at the table.

'Is your shoulder bleeding, Rocco?' I asked, noticing

that it was slightly lower and more hunched than the other, making his body unsymmetrical. I went behind him and helped him take his shirt off, easing the material over his bad shoulder, where there was a slight kidney-shaped bruise, with a scab of blood that was already drying into dark solid shapes like mould. The bruise was turning a heavy shade of purple, but he moved his shoulder up and down to show me it didn't hurt.

'It's fine,' he said, and I touched his neck with my finger comfortingly in circles over his soft skin, watching a bit of colour come back into his cheeks, feeling ambivalent towards my brother in the half-light.

'Let's call a doctor, Rocco,' I said, nodding my head in the direction of the body on our sofa. 'I'll say he fell.' I ran my cold fingers over the corner of the board where the moths were stuck, feeling anxious as if the moths were inside my tummy and trying to escape. Their jewel abdomens were cracking slightly on the board, aging under the sharp pins, but they were still very straight and elegant. I peeled a splinter of wood off the corner and rolled it around between my fingers, letting the sharp ends nudge the tips of my fingers for a moment without piercing the skin.

'Let's wait a couple of hours, if he doesn't wake up, we'll phone,' Rocco said, holding my arm. I nodded and Rocco closed the medical book. A piece of tissue blotched with inky blood was lying by my hand to the right and the very deep, almost brown liquid was the same colour as one of the rippled eyes on a little grey-bodied moth.

'Do you want a cup of tea?' Rocco said and I shrugged. 'You watch Jackson, make sure you don't move him and call me if he wakes up. I'm going to go make tea.'

There were two great knots of tension on either side of my neck, heavy seeds growing under my skin and I shivered as I looked at Jackson lying on our sofa. His black shirt was sweaty and crumpled over his chest and under his arms, his hair sticking up slightly in different directions. The television was still on with the sound down, but as light began to creep through the windows into the room, the blue tinge of the screen wasn't as noticeable as it had been before Jackson arrived. The nature programme about penguins was over and a garden show had begun, demonstrating how to make wooden patios. I looked briefly at Jackson, who still had his heavy eyelids closed and a trickle of blood climbing out of him, but then turned to watch the television until Rocco came in with breakfast.

Time became very slow and frozen in the house with Jackson lying on the sofa. He woke up while we were drinking tea and eating dried chocolate Rice Krispies from the packet, but he didn't know where he was and when he tried to speak, his words were jumbled together and mumbled.

I remembered how Jackson used to come over to my house on Saturday mornings and we'd watch television. He'd keep his hand on the dents of my knee, which made me nervous at first until I got used to his touch. I remembered his totally lazy expressions and the difficulty with which I understood the subtle difference between his sarcasm and his genuine affection.

'Thank God,' Rocco said. 'He's getting better,' but I wasn't sure. Rocco wouldn't let me answer the telephone when it rang. He said that if it were Jackson's parents then we'd have to explain what happened and it would be better to let him get better before telling them that he'd hit his head. Rocco said we needed time to plead with Jackson, to explain the scenario, which made sense, and anyway, I didn't want them to come into the house. I imagined the disgust and confusion on their faces as they saw the mess and mayhem of the sitting room and I imagined their questions, their expressions, the tone of their voices. The thoughts made my heart begin to race again, so I let the phone ring off as Jackson mumbled and groaned, and I touched his head. The blood had stopped oozing from the back of his skull, which appeared to be a sign of improvement, but his forehead felt hotter than it had been before. We thought of giving him aspirin, but he wouldn't swallow anything, so Rocco took them instead for the ache in his arm.

Rocco moved the sculpture of the eye from the loft and he fiddled with it distractedly, slotting it together and running his fingers over the smooth skin of its lightly painted body while I played with the mouse. There was a great photograph of a head in the medical book, showing the sluggish wrinkles of the brain inside, different shades of white in blotches from the ultrasound and Rocco ripped it out to pin on the mantelpiece. It was full of swirls and curls of heat and light, all encased in the skull like a magic Pandora's box. The phone rang again, around mid-day and again we ignored it, disliking the noise for disturbing the bubble of the house.

'You know Chatterton?' Rocco said, and I shook my head. 'He was a poet,' he said, and I shrugged, wondering where he learnt all these things. Until last year, I'd still thought that the Romantic poets were mythical storybook characters like Merlin. 'He wrote six hundred pages of verse, two tragedies, one finished and one not, and a burletta. He committed suicide before he turned eighteen.' Rocco was staring at the television blankly and quite sadly I thought. The walls seemed to be tightening the air.

'Any good?' I asked, knowing from Rocco's expression that my brother obviously thought Chatterton was good. Jackson squirmed.

'People used to argue about whether he was just a forger and a delinquent, because he pretended that some of his poetry was written by a medieval man called Thomas Rowley, or if he was a child genius.'

'And which is he?' I asked and Rocco shrugged.

'It would be nice to find out. One day, when I'm older, I want to write a book about him. Everyone's forgotten about him.' I watched Rocco's blank, tired face. On the television there was now a show about the making of Disney cartoons, mostly just boring people sitting in chairs talking, cut up by brief interludes of characters rushing after each other, without any background.

'Three times the virgin, swimming on the breeze,' Rocco quoted, and then paused. Jackson moved on the sofa next to us, perhaps trying to curl up, but he couldn't.

'Is he getting better?' I asked Rocco and he shrugged.

'I guess,' he said. 'He's moving.'

Jackson's eyes began to roll slightly in his head, his pupils huge and sea-worn granite pebbles. Then suddenly he was squirming on the sofa in front of us, his cheeks flaming, his hair glowing with fat drops of sweat at its tips, holding himself and scaring me. The walls were smaller, the air tighter and Rocco looked nervous. He had none of the stern calm that he usually possessed. His eyes were jumpy and he wasn't telling me what he was actually thinking. I could almost feel Jackson's heat, but Rocco was pretending to be unalarmed.

'Call an ambulance, Rocco,' I said stiffly.

'He's going to be fine,' Rocco replied.

'Look at him,' I said, the pitch of my voice rising, pointing at the sweat all over his face and the blood on the pillow. 'Call an ambulance.'

Rocco refused, his hand shaking slightly. I repeated my plea once more, louder, and then Rocco leaned over to the one phone line in the house and cut it with a pair of scissors sitting next to a broken plate on the floor. I moved to stop him, but the action was so jagged and quick that my movement was useless and the line was cut. I didn't look at him as he told me it would get him in too much trouble, reminding me it was him at stake not me. This separation struck me deeply, carefully, and precisely. I had not brought this on, I was not the one who was deciding not to get a doctor. Again, I was a bystander to drama and I did not understand. I suppose Rocco was scared, not thinking straight, and I tried to breathe deeply. There was some colour in Jackson's cheeks, but I had a feeling it was just colour from the heat of his fever and I held his hand, which was clammy, and he didn't seem even to know who I was, scaring me.

I wanted out. If this was Rocco's drama, which he seemed to have made it, then I didn't want to be a player. I still remembered Jackson's touch, lips on lips, hands on skin. Perhaps I just wanted to be out of the house, or perhaps away from Rocco's mournful eyes, or Jackson's heavy breathing and painful movements, but certainly I wanted fresh air and time to think about what I was going to do, so I suggested that perhaps Jackson might want some food now, knowing we had nothing in the house. Rocco sensed my uneasiness and offered to go out and buy some but I answered abruptly that I wanted to, because if Jackson got worse while Rocco was away I wouldn't know what to do. Rocco watched me, looking me in the eye with every limb in his big body, scared that this was it. Then he nodded.

—ɯ—

OUTSIDE

I had my passport, a wad of notes and the mouse in my pocket when I left. It was even colder outside than in the house. It felt good to be away from the stifling smell of blood and water in the living room. Camden was drying out again after having been briefly sweetened by snow, and grit kept launching itself off the pavement and into my wide eyes, making them water as I walked down the afternoon streets. The snow had also stripped parts of Camden bare, but the mouse was warm in my pocket. There were geometric rivets of dirt where I was sure that there used to be fat London trees, and the dirt that had survived was muddled up with cigarettes and splintered polystyrene cups. The bricks were a hundred different dull reds, crawling with moss, and there were cracked windows, homes held up by scaffolding, and broken walls. A woman with a green raincoat and frizzy hair parked her bicycle for a moment at the traffic lights and squinted at me through her glasses, short-sighted maybe and absently scanning the crowds before moving on. There were groups of young girls and boys, tasting their first lonely excitement in the crowds of the colourful London market.

I walked past a mirror shop and was shocked by the ten reflections of my face. I had all of my long hair piled up in Rocco's hat and I looked like a strange bug-eyed boy, wearing Dad's cashmere jumper and a pair of baggy trousers. My eyes were out of proportion without my hair to frame them, my long mouth twitched slightly and that sexless doll reflection was repeated over and over again in the glass. The pavement beneath my feet was uneven, as if a big earthworm had made its slow way underneath, pushing the cement blocks around as it arched and flexed. The walls around were painted with loud graffiti, the gawping mouths of the clothes shops spitting leather bags and shoes into my path.

The supermarket was shut, because it was Sunday, so I walked towards the river where Dad's shop and a lot of little grocery shops were. I began to get nervous, my brow creasing as I approached the store, and I kept my eyes downcast at the pavement, stepping carefully over crushed chips, cigarette buts and soggy club leaflets. I stood outside the shop, which had all the

blinds pulled down over the dirty windows so that I
had to crouch down with my knees against my breasts
in order to see. It was empty and dark inside, all the
antiques gone, leaving a gloomy blank television
screen. The counter was still there, sticking up at the
back and there were hooks on the walls where the
guns used to hang. As my eyes got accustomed to the
light I noticed that the guns had left their shadows in
their home, faint areas of lighter paint, which had
been covered up by guns for so many years. There
were a couple of cans of Coke in the corner, perhaps
left by the men who had cleared out the shop, and a
plastic bag was wavering in the draft from underneath
the door, shifting from side to side. It grew as it moved
away from the door and shivered as it crawled back.
My hands were on the dirty pavement to keep me
balanced, locked in sweaty fists so that only my stern
knuckles were becoming indented by the sandpaper
texture of the damp pavement.

When we had been sitting on our new neighbours'
roof, Rocco said I was living in the halfway house
wasteland of being sixteen, sitting on the edge. I felt
now that the entire wasteland had crumbled upwards
like cigarette smoke, showing me this vile picture. I
wondered if Rocco had seen the picture years ago, or
at least a suspect outline. Rocco and I had spent the
last five years huddled inside our own heads, aware of
every shift and every self-obsessed emotion while our

father had been disintegrating. I remembered how thin he got, his translucent skin and spots, his yellow nails, tired eyes, slow movements, flu, constant coughing, and I wondered how I could have been so wrapped up in myself and my brother.

Parents are the source of all understanding for children. They could have told us that darkness was inside-out light and the universe was a huge eggshell and we would have believed them. So Mum, the source of all knowledge, keeper of trust, told us that Dad had flu and we believed her.

I moved one arm up to the ledge and didn't look behind me, although it seemed as if everyone was looking at me. Rocco and I used to play a game where we would draw a tree by filling in only the empty areas between the branches with our black crayons, so we'd get a backwards picture. The empty shop made me think of a backwards space, turned violently inside out by some huge gust of wind. My hair, piled under Rocco's hat, was hot even in the cold, and my eyes felt as if they were perspiring, heavy with treacle, sugary and stinging under their eyelid hood. I didn't blink, but stared at the drained shop for another long moment before taking the mouse out of my pocket and stroking her for the last time. I put her on the floor and she looked up at me with her red eyes.

'Lots of rubbish in London,' I said, but the mouse didn't move. Then something seemed to catch its attention behind me and it scurried off towards it, leaving me crouching outside what used to be Dad's shop, feeling sad. I ought to have called an ambulance, but within the bustle of Camden town it seemed inconceivable that Jackson would die. He'd hit his head. Lots of people hit their heads.

My toe caught itself on a wet cobblestone as I got up and began to move off, but I avoided falling down and drifted off into the crowd. The narrow streets of the inner market were joined together by wet crowded corridors, each lined with doors leading into shallow shops. I slid between the tourists and the jewellery stalls, pushing and grunting, and as my hand glided across the wall, I could feel the sludge of old moss between my fingers. I felt lost, which was strange because I knew Camden so well, but I shoved through the back alleys, past a horde of Chinese tourists, through some gothic school girls, and into a courtyard space where I stood behind a broken writing desk sitting on the pavement and searched the crowd for the colour red.

I found the colour of blood and sunsets and fire in the dress of a female dummy perched outside a shop with a pole up her skirt and a chain around her neck. She had wide plastic eyes and the pink skin of her armless shoulder sockets were peeling to reveal a rusting green-tinted metal. I also saw the colour red in some foreign graffiti on the wall opposite, a sign advertising a break dance show starting next week, and a dress in the window of a shop. I began to speed up and knocked over the naked body of a plastic torso with a pink curly wig on its divine looking face. The plastic man looked as if he had travelled in time and should have been opening the first Olympics rather than advertising wigs in Camden market, a disenchanted, strange look on his plastic face. He fell with a clatter and a clank on to the cobbled stones, face first, and stayed there ignominiously on the wet cobbles, unable to get up again.

There was a flower stall, a shop offering bondage equipment, and then a stall of Venetian masks. Everything was hiding behind something, layers and layers of market, and the dummies scattered in fancy dress around the streets reminded me of the toy soldiers back in the safety of our loft, full of potential but stuck in their lifeless perfect bodies. Each dummy had a different face and character, but was the same armless and legless corpse. I could feel the cold post-snow air come out of my mouth in white steamed milk bundles. My chest was rising, falling, and the whole market was heaving and feverish, jumping from very hot to horribly cold without warning. The red ribbons dangling from the signs above one of the shop displays, the neon white of a 20s-style dress and the green shirt of the man who was minding the shop next to where I was standing, were all hiding me with their gaudy lights. The sky in a thin road above my head was grey as the scar tissue on my wrist and Rocco's nose.

My fist was clenched into a solid ball and my wrist was bulging with blood wires. My legs were soft and filled with liquid air, which was slowly deflating and letting helium fizz into my head. The people in the market connected as if the city was one organic, living, breathing animal, each bit feeding off another aspect and working together like the human body. It wasn't spectacle, it wasn't fake, it was alive and I felt suffocated. I had an image of Dad in my head that I couldn't blank out. He was sitting on a slab of concrete somewhere, wearing a dirty linen shirt and pale trousers, watching river water speed by underneath him. I couldn't see his face, but I expect he had a vacuous and lost look. I imagined there were a lot of people around him, but he wasn't in London. I simply felt hopelessly numb and metallic, toy-soldier-like and hungry.

Walking through the streets where Rocco and I had created so many memories – the video store, the Chinese takeaway, the park benches where we sat and ate chips from greasy paper and watched Camden shuffle by in front of us – I reminded myself of how it had always felt like us against the entire adult world. Rocco hadn't betrayed me by not telling me when he worked out about Dad, he'd only tried to save me. If I abandoned Rocco now I would crush our past into fairy dust. More than anything, more even than reality, happiness, practicality or morality, I loved him. I could spend the money on some sort of education, finish my exams, get a boyfriend. I'd leave and find a job, lead a normal life, but Rocco wouldn't be in it and I couldn't stand the idea of him not being the one to wake me up in the morning. I was dependent, if you like, as I'd always been, for better or for worse.

The terrible thing is that I didn't even half-betray him, I didn't even call a doctor. I went into a grocery store instead and bought two big bags of food.

I took a final breath of fresh air when at last I somehow found myself on our doorstep and opened the door as if I was diving into water. I took Rocco's black hat off my head, letting my hair fall down over my shoulders, smelling of wool and damp sweat. The air was so cold that I was almost breathing white. Rocco was looking at the ceiling in the sitting room and I stared at him. As every city sound rang out in the padded cold, we both blinked. He looked more relieved to see my face than I'd ever seen him look before, air sighing out from his big shoulders and a faint, conciliatory smile softened his scared face for a moment. I took the food out of the plastic bag and put it down on the coffee table next to Rocco, whose face was blank and white.

'He doesn't seem to be getting better. He's not conscious again,' Rocco said, putting Jackson's floppy hand on what was now a pile of most of the blankets in the house sitting on top of Jackson. Rocco put his head in his hands, running his fingers through the curls.

Rocco picked up one of the soldiers and fiddled around with it in his hand, sadly.

'What do we do then?' I snapped, and we paused. Jackson wasn't tossing or groaning anymore, but lying very still with his eyes open, his breathing rougher. I began to plait my hair, but it came undone again as it always did. I passed Rocco a chocolate bar and he ate it mechanically while watching Jackson out of the corner of his eye.

Rocco's face was half-drawn over by shadow, his wide eyes puffy and dark from lack of sleep. I could hear the muffled sounds of cars and people out on the street, but much more powerful was the sound of Jackson's breathing filling up the room. I sat down, feeling drained and hopeless. Rocco lit a cigarette and put it in front of his green eyes to look me over, then he spun it on its side and looked at me again from a different angle. I wanted Rocco to come and sit next to me, to share the warmth of his cigarette and his body with me. If I had been eight and he had been ten again, if none of this had happened, he would have sat next to me on the cold wooden floor, sharing his cigarette and touching me. But even together again now, there were fine scars.

—⚊—

24

TIME

We slept badly that night, taking turns to watch Jackson breathe in the dark. Rocco should have gone to work but instead I offered to cook a proper breakfast with eggs and tomatoes and bacon. Mum had taught me to cook breakfast when I was eleven, one day during the summer holidays when we were always demanding meals. First I put oil in a pan over the stove, letting it boil before peeling away the thin streaky bits of pink bacon from the greasy packaging and placing them on top so that they rode the oil for a moment and then sunk under. I whisked up egg and milk, dipping bread in and fried it in another pan so that the smell of yolk and grease began to fill up the house, the sounds of fizzing oil breaking the silence. I fried half worlds of tomatoes till they were soft and gooey inside, buttered the toast and laid the table. I felt Rocco needed looking after.

We ate in silence, hungry and tired, but felt slightly more comforted afterwards than we had done before, even though Jackson was still not moving in the sitting room.

I padded around the house for an hour or so while Rocco sat in the sitting room. I opened the back door to get the thick smell of fried bacon and butter out of the house and wished Mum and Dad would come home, innocent again, perhaps like they were just after I was born.

I went upstairs to the loft and started to search for a yellow dress Mum had bought me for my birthday last year, which I'd never worn because it was too much the sort of dress that suited Mum, with a square neck, little flowers all over it and buttons down the front. It had a belt in the middle that tied in a bow at the back. I took a blue jumper off the floor, where it had been sitting in a crumpled heap next to a grey T-shirt with stains down it that I used to wear all the time when I was thirteen. There were some sandals with broken buckles and fraying straw heels, tennis shoes and a pink bra. The whole wardrobe seemed full of absurd things like teddy bears and Rocco's old school uniform with its tatty frayed cuffs and dirty hemlines.

I began to hurl more things on to the floor, kicking stuff that got caught up in my feet backwards into a pile. There were some of Rocco's books with their spines snapped and I hurled them out, looking for the dress. On the shelf above the wardrobe were piles of old magazines snowed over with grey dust, and another frozen moth took its last flight with the magazines to the floor, but the dress wasn't there. I found a copy of *Alice in Wonderland*, old textbooks, and artwork underneath the table, empty water bottles, and exam study guides, but no yellow dress.

I pulled viciously at Rocco's bed, knocking the pigeon on to the floor where it looked mournfully up at me from the corner of the room and huddled itself to watch. The yellow dress was there, behind the bed where I had hidden it last year so that I didn't have to wear it. It was a pretty dress, made out of very soft silky material just like I remembered against my cheek when I wouldn't let go of Mum's leg to go to pre-school. I took off all my clothes, fumbling with the zip of the trousers and tugging to rip my hair from the neck of the jumper. I wiped my eyes with bacon smelling hands and stood there, freezing and naked for a moment before pulling the dress over my body. Already, before it happened, I felt tearful and ready, my body sticky and aching, my eyes stinging.

Downstairs Rocco was asleep and Jackson's face had turned from very red to a white colour that matched one of Dad's white china eggs fallen from the mantelpiece. I went over to stand above the sofa and watched the very faint breathing, just a minute amount of air skimming through his scorched, blue-tinted lips. They were slightly cracked in the centre like the bodies of the moths. I went over and kneeled down beside him, the silky yellow folds of the dress folding over my thighs, and I held Jackson's hand. It was cold and wet, the back of his wrist where all the blood wires were packed had flattened slightly, the skin even thinner than it had been before. All his fingers were limp as he died in front of me, his pulse stuttering and pausing, his lips quivering for a moment and then absolutely nothing.

I didn't even cry; it was such a shock to see a dead body lying covered in duvets on our sofa. He had a vacant expression on his face, his eyes were closed, his lips blue and he didn't look like Jackson at all, but like a waxwork in a museum, something we'd stolen.

When I looked round, Rocco had woken up and was also seeing what I was seeing, his face almost as white as Jackson's. I let go of Jackson's hand and placed it on top of the pile of duvets very softly. Neither Rocco nor I said anything for a moment and then Rocco took a breath as if he hadn't been breathing for the last ten minutes as Jackson died in front of us.

The house smelt, the walls felt as if they were falling inwards, the furniture was everywhere, the antiques broken or stolen, and the pile of duvets on the sofa was eerily still. The walls were closed as a box around us, all angular and muffled. The television was still faltering its pretty images on the screen and clipping Mum and Dad's remaining possessions with the tinted light. It was as if every mistake we'd ever made had been sucked into the little painted eggs Mum used to collect and then hatched out, new and covered in hot milk-coloured foetal liquid. And so there we were, in the same room that Rocco used to sit in, silently drinking tea, our palms in our laps, while our parents entertained guests, except now something empty was lying on the sofa where we used to sit.

'We have to go,' Rocco said sharply, fear suddenly brightening his hooded eyes. 'Shit, I've . . . I was just reading and I looked up and his eyes were all . . .' he trailed off and looked at Jackson again. 'I've actually . . .' but he couldn't say it. 'We have to go now, Isabel.' Rocco looked to see what I was going to do, to see how sure my previous decision had been, but I suppose I looked unusually tranquil. Rocco got up and pulled the duvet over Jackson's head, his hands shaking with terribly fine, slithery movement. Rocco's whole body had turned in a moment from solid, to being pure liquid, melting and fermenting now so that he couldn't stand, but had to sit down on the coffee table, unable to move his eyes from the pile of duvets on the bed. He kept saying the words 'I've actually . . .' and then trailing off. He lit a cigarette, but his hand was shaking too much and he put it out on the floor. 'We have to go,' he repeated. 'We have to go now,' but I couldn't move and remained hovering above the sofa.

'He fell,' I said limply, my hands hanging at my side, my body cold. Rocco said something under his breath and he looked so sad, his hands fidgeting with each other on his lap, his skin flushed, the bruise on his arm getting larger. It's terrible, but there wasn't even a moment when I contemplated our confessing.

'I didn't mean . . .' Rocco began, trailing off again like his words were getting sucked into the mayhem of the house. 'Oh,' he said. There was the bag of money and a few clothes in the corner of the room, which we'd taken from Jackson's house and I shakily put the sculpture of the eye and the four soldiers into the bag with our passports. Rocco didn't watch me, but instead stared at the piled-up sofa.

Rocco and I both sat down, him on the floor and me on the table, and for an hour the only sign that he was dead and we were alive were the sounds of our heavy breathing in the quiet. I didn't have a single thought in my head. After a while I got up and went to the kitchen. I washed up a mug and turned on the tap, pouring myself a glass of cold water. I turned round and leaned on the sink to drink it, watching the curtains of the window crease up and down in the snowy wind from the open window. My skin was white too, especially the palm of my hand, made of pasted together snowflakes. I dipped my fingers in the water and put a few drops on my wrist, letting the little bubbles roll down my arm, then I washed up two more glasses and filled them with water to bring into the sitting room. I put one of the glasses in my brother's hand and the other next to Jackson's body on the table.

I looked at my watch and it was five in the evening, so I estimated that he had probably died at three-thirty. The blood on the pillow under his head was beginning to scab and bruise the material, clinging to his hair as if it were gluing him to the sofa, making Jackson a part of the house, mindless now. I suppose that the chemicals in his brain were giving up their desperate drive to send messages of pain and pleasure, his nerves loosening their eighteen-year grip against each other. I imagined that the bright muscles, which had been so tightly gift-wrapped over the bones of his toes and his fingers, were moving to open now, softly, quietly, like flowers in the morning. He had no pulse, so I suppose the purple blood simply stopped in the tunnels of his arteries and veins, letting all the nutrients he had eaten that day stultify in stomach pockets. Alcohol from his Friday night fun and some sort of drug probably still inside him. I heard once that fingernails continue to grow for days after a person dies, so everything moving in his body must have been creeping up through the joints of his fingers to finish this one last job before switching off all the lights in the factory, shutting down the machinery. I felt as if he wasn't quite nothing yet, not quite earth and ashes, not Jackson anymore but an alien, statuesque piece of organic cold-climate coral grown in our house.

While Rocco was still sitting with his head in his hands, I went upstairs and washed my hair. It was too hot and the steamy water burnt my skin, but the shampoo smelt of lemon, heavy as white treacle against my tight skin and it sent a shiver down every puzzle-piece in my spine. I imagined the motorway of Jackson's body empty now from messages, and after I was saturated and clean I dried myself off on a Minnie Mouse towel that was lying in a heap in the corner of the tiled room. I then took a pair of scissors from a cup and carefully cut my hair to my shoulders, letting big wet auburn chunks fall into the sink. I tried not to think about the fact that I had let him die and now I was washing my hair, I just thought about the long damp hair filling up the white sink.

I looked down at my body, red from the hot water and I felt the bump of my tummy, my belly button, the sickly shadows under my breasts, the bones of my shoulders and the tight muscles in my heavy neck. I closed my eyes in front of the frosted circular mirror, listening to the crashing sound of shower water on the plastic floor behind me. I opened my eyes and turned off the shower, then dried my hair roughly with the towel. Then I put my clothes back on and wrapped my hair up in a bundle.

When I came out of the bathroom I jumped at the sight of Rocco, tears making rivets in his face for the first time since he was ten and fell off a tree. He was carrying Jackson and the duvets in his arms up the stairs.

'What are you doing?' I snapped at him.

'I don't know,' Rocco faltered.

'Well, put him down,' I snapped.

'Here?' he answered, straining under the dead weight.

'Why did you move him?' I asked, my voice different and strange, the towel untangling itself from my hair.

'I don't know. Jesus, we can't just leave him there.'

'Well, where *can* we leave him?' I said desperately, my head violently blank. I took the towel off from my head and let it fall to the floor next to my feet while I opened the door to Mum and Dad's bedroom, where I stood for a moment. But the sight of the dysfunctional, chaotic room with all of their spoiled things piled up made me feel as if I was about to throw up, so I closed the door again.

'What does it matter where he is?' I said. 'He's dead. Dead upstairs, dead in the hallway, dead downstairs.'

'Upstairs?' he said.

'Fine,' I said. I opened the door to the loft for Rocco to walk in, stepping careful as a dancer over the soldiers and clothes on the floor. The pigeon was sitting on the windowsill, it's bubble eyes glistening as it half-watched us. It continued to preen its grey feathers with its dirty beak as Rocco put the body down on the bed, still wrapped tightly in his damp blanket coffin. The pigeon jumped from the windowsill, as if it had intended to fly but was too fat, and landed on the floor of the loft. I made a sharp movement with my hands and scared it out of the window where it flew up to its chimney home.

'I think we should get away. Let's catch a train,' I said.

25

—ᘓᘏ—

THE LAST CHAPTER

There are no fat, violent pigeons watching us now we live away from London. There is no Jackson, no nervous parents and nobody pounding on our door. This new city needs to be rained on because the air is heavy with liquid, the sky plump and gooey. The window of our room is open and there is water jumping out of the drain in the alley below, making me terribly thirsty. Above the tall block in front I can just see a wound of sky cut up by television antennae and the clouds are low against the roofs. It's almost as if there is a shopping bag of water above the buildings, which is stretching slowly lower and lower, ready to break and rain over all of us. For the moment, everybody is sitting around waiting for a downpour, feeling sticky. The flats opposite are so close that we can see everything inside: a woman eating pasta by herself in a neat, sparse kitchen, and above her an old lady watching television.

Rocco is reading on our bed behind me, but I can see a slight reflection of him in the glass of the slanted window, so I know that he keeps looking up. I am wearing my new short brown hair up at the moment and Rocco is staring at my neck, his head cocked thoughtfully to the side as if he were trying to remember something profound or sinister. Down on the street at the very edge of the alley there is a bench where tanned girls are chatting and boys are parking their mopeds. The charming, blurred chatter, mixed with pop music, is filtering up through the heat, and it needs desperately to rain before anyone will be able to breathe again.

Rocco's hand lands softly on my neck and I notice that evening is pushing a black mesh over Paris. I begin to scratch the old varnish from the corner of the desk with the nail of my middle finger, feeling restless and hot as an insomniac child, twitching the shiny layers away till they peel in flakes off the side. There is the slight burden now of having to nurse the lingering child inside me. It is a strong, wilful, spoilt child who will not go to bed when it's told or bite its tongue in awkward situations. It sits peaceful sometimes for days, and then embarks without warning on moody tantrums which sometimes fill our whole room, and the smell of adrenaline and sweet child sweat seeps out of the window into the alley. Rocco is less babyish, less exhilarated now, his mouth a little bit tighter around the edges like Dad's, but his eyes are still wide and moist as they had been as a child when he used to make Mum nervous with his thoughtful watching.

He's stroking my neck now, and the touch of his hand on my skin gives me a sudden fit of helpless yawning. I am sitting with my head cocked to the side, the softness of my cheek just touching his hand and I am yawning like a bored cat on a tin roof. I can see both our figures in the reflection from the glass of the window, looking simultaneously dazed with slight weariness. I can see him watching me, feel his large fingers run across my collarbone and I allow his hand to rest on my skin, with his fingers between the curves of my breasts.

I thought that perhaps we might fight tonight, over anything – or nothing – just because we were too hot and tired. However, while I yawn he is grinning at my reflection in the glass and the water above the city has suddenly broken. At first the scattering is uncertain and then the water blooms into full-out rain, the steamy and clean kind, as if crows are descending from a fairy tale on to our window, or hot metal soldiers are dropping from the sky.